The Diary of Samuel Newton, Alderman of Cambridge, 1662-1717

Samuel Newton

The Diary of Samuel Newton, Alderman of Cambridge, 1662-1717

ISBN/EAN: 9783337015541

Printed in Europe, USA, Canada, Australia, Japan

Cover: Foto ©Raphael Reischuk / pixelio.de

More available books at **www.hansebooks.com**

THE DIARY

OF

SAMUEL NEWTON

ALDERMAN OF CAMBRIDGE

(1662—1717)

EDITED BY

J. E. FOSTER, M.A.,
TRINITY COLLEGE.

Cambridge:
PRINTED FOR THE CAMBRIDGE ANTIQUARIAN SOCIETY.
SOLD BY DEIGHTON, BELL, AND CO., AND
MACMILLAN AND CO.
1890

Cambridge:
PRINTED BY C. J. CLAY, M.A. AND SONS,
AT THE UNIVERSITY PRESS.

PREFACE.

ANTIQUARIANS connected with Cambridge will be well aware that its municipal history has been fully told by the late Mr Charles Henry Cooper, Town Clerk, in his *Annals of Cambridge*. The *Diary* of Alderman Newton did not escape his notice; and he has used it as his authority for many facts during the period to which it refers. Extracts from it will be familiar to the reader of the *Annals*.

It has been thought, however, that a complete copy of the *Diary* would be worth printing, as the minor facts referred to were not of sufficient interest to be mentioned in the *Annals*; and also because it contains many entries of purely domestic interest which should be put on record for the use of enquirers into family history.

The *Diary* is in the Library of Downing College, among the MSS bequeathed by Mr John Bowtell. It is written in the latter portion of a thin folio volume, in other portions of which are copies of forms used in the municipal business of the town, probably entered by the Alderman himself for his personal use. The handwriting varies a good deal; in parts it is very good, and in others equally bad.

The authorities of the College were good enough to permit the removal of the MS from their library for transcription, for which favour many thanks are due. A similar debt is due to the two ladies who did the greater part of the transcribing; to Mr Bullen of Barnard Castle, and to other friends, for information on various points connected with the facts and persons referred to in the *Diary*; while the somewhat troublesome task of collating the proofs with the original was thrown upon the late Editor to the Society, the present Librarian of the University.

1 *May*, 1890.

⁎ In printing the Journal, words and phrases which have been written in afterwards are put in italics; words and phrases which have been erased are included between asterisks.

INTRODUCTION.

THE family of the writer of the following Diary seems now to have died out in this district, though it was at one time rather important.

A genealogy of the family, with a trick of their arms, is contained in the Heralds Visitation of Cambridge in 1684, authenticated by the signature of Samuel Newton, writer of the Diary. According to it the family originally sprang from Newcastle on Tyne, and its first representative in this County was John Newton, who was minister of Bourne, and died in 1610, leaving a son John, who is described as a "limner," and who died in 1635. He married the daughter of a Hales, and from the fact that John Newton is described as an artist, it may be conjectured that Mr Hales was the father of the well-known artist who flourished in the reign of Charles II., and painted the portrait of Pepys the Diarist. It is unfortunate that the records at both Christ's College and Bourne are deficient at the period of the decease of John Newton the father, and that it is not possible, apparently, to find out the date of the birth of John Newton the son, or who his mother was. His description as a "limner" might enable us to add an artist of local reputation to the scanty list of English artists of this date; but he was apparently unknown to fame, as there is no mention of him in Walpole's *Anecdotes*, nor in other lists of English Artists so far as researches can be made.

The family appears to have died out, at all events of Cambridge, shortly after the date to which the genealogy is brought down in the visitation record.

The prominent and handsome tomb of Sarah Newton, daughter of Samuel Newton the younger, stated in the genealogy to be his only child and aged two years, is no doubt a familiar object to members of the Society and visitors to Cambridge, standing as it does in the church-yard attached to St Benet's Church, and not far from the foot of the steps leading from the street. The tomb will be more familiar to visitors as being adorned with the well-known Newton arms, two shin-bones in saltire, so well known to all Cambridge men as being those borne by Sir Isaac Newton. It is unfortunate, however, that there seems to have been no connection between the families. Copies of the pedigree of Sir Isaac Newton are contained in Turner's *Collections for the History of Grantham*, and in the *Miscellanea Genealogica et Heraldica*, as has been pointed out to me by Dr Edleston, but there seems to be no connection with this family; and it is only possible to suppose that the heralds of that day granted the same arms to all families having the same surnames, without troubling themselves to enquire whether they sprang from the same root or not.

The diary contains many entries of great interest, both to local antiquarians, and to students of the more widely extended fields of both municipal and general civil laws and customs.

Among the many entries relating to local topography the first to catch the eye is the reference to the Cross on Market Hill. This stood on a site nearly opposite to the present door of the Guildhall. It is believed to have been destroyed in the year 1764, when its place was taken by the conduit supplied by water from Hobson's Stream, which many of my readers will remember as standing there previous to its removal to the north end of Trumpington Road, where it now stands. The pillory which also stood close to the same spot, and is referred to in the diary under the date of March 11, 166$\frac{4}{5}$, was removed within the memory of some of the older inhabitants of Cambridge.

The reference in the year 1660 to the admission of Newton's sister and wife to booths in Sturbridge Fair will recall the value then attached to these in Cambridge. The number of booths and the extent of space they occupied was strictly limited, considerable sums were given for the privilege of having one, and a large annual rental accrued therefrom. Many plans of the fair are extant, shewing the manner in which the space was apportioned amongst the various trades, and reminiscences of these still remain in some of the streets and lanes on the site. In the account of the proclamation of the fair on the 7th September, 1668, the parts called the Duddery, Goldsmiths' Row, Bookbinders' Row, the Water fayre, and Honey Hill, are mentioned; and in the entry of the 12th January, 166$\frac{8}{9}$, that of the Hop Fair, the only industry which still retains in a very slight way the commercial character of the fair.

At the N. E. corner of Sturbridge Green lies the piece of ground referred to in the diary as "Bullins" under the date of the 23rd March, 166$\frac{4}{5}$. The depositions in certain law-suits relating to it which took place in 1668 are preserved in the Record Office[1]. These suits seem to have arisen between the occupiers and owners and the purchasers of the tithes late belonging to the Priory of Barnwell, the owners contending that the lands were tithe-free. The metes and bounds accordingly are carefully stated in the evidence given by the various witnesses, from which the exact situation of this plot may be determined, and it will be found to correspond to the piece of ground now occupied as an osier-holt adjacent to the railway-bridge over the river Cam, and bounded by the river

---

[1] Fortieth *Report* of the Keeper of the Public Records (1879), pp. 168, 240, 357.

on the north. Subsequently it had acquired the name of Boulogne, evidently a corruption of the ancient name. At the time of the diarist, a house of entertainment seems to have stood on it, a probable enough fact from its proximity to the fair, and also because it was in the hands of others than the Corporation, who were owners of the fair, and therefore doubtless jealous of their privileges in it, and charging high rents to taverners who occupied booths there.

Reach Fair, referred to under the 1st May, 1665, was doubtless a more important source of revenue to the Corporation than it is now, though the members of the Corporation still attend in state, and the tolls collected go into its coffers. These do not now cover the cost of the conveyance of those members of the Corporation who attend, but the position of the village, on the high land just at the edge of the fen, would make it in earlier days an important centre of traffic. According to the entry on the 17th May, 1669, such members of the Corporation as chose to attend rode to the fair, and the horse used by the Mayor was adorned with handsome harness, a somewhat incongruous arrangement, one would have supposed, for a 12 miles ride through the then unmade bridle paths leading to the fens. It is hardly necessary to state that Reach lies at the north end of the great dyke called the Devil's Ditch, which was thrown up in very early days, possibly as a tribal division, and extended from the edge of the fens at Reach to the woodlands of Woodditton, passing across Newmarket Heath, on which the Ditch Mile is a well known portion of the racecourse. The fair is held on a piece of common ground which lies just at the end of the Dyke, and is thought to have originated from a market which was held there as being neutral ground.

It is a matter of surprise to find under the date of the 20 November, 1666, that one of the Aldermen of the Town was married to the widow of another member of that body in King's College Chapel. As the present site of the College was not at that time occupied as such, but the whole of the frontage was occupied by houses, the chapel may have been looked on as more of a parish-church than it is now; but there seems to have been no connection between the parties and the College to account for such a deviation from the usual practice[1].

The foundation of his school by Stephen Perse appears to have been appreciated by the inhabitants of the town; for, if the school had not been thought good, a man in the position of the diarist would not have entered his son there, as it will be observed he did on the 12th February, 166⅞. At this time the Master of Gonville and Caius College evidently had more direct control over the School than is vested in his hands now, as an order was obtained from him for the admission of the new scholar.

The notice of the butter-market under the date of 7th March, 1666, will recall to those who knew the Town before recent changes, how the arches under the present front of the Guildhall were occupied by the dealers in that article, though they have now been removed to the opposite side of the market-place. The passage which goes round that part of the building is still called Butter Row.

The account of the funeral of Matthew Wren, Bishop of Ely, and uncle of the great architect, is full of interest, as it contains such a minute description of the manner in which such solemnities were carried out. Readers of the *Diary of Henry Machyn*, published by the Camden Society, will remember how full that is of accounts of similar ceremonies at a period about 100 years earlier. The form of ceremony seems to have been very similar at both periods, shewing the same strong conservative tendencies amongst the actors on such occasions as still exists. The great prominence given to the heraldic insignia is noticeable, and other examples of it occur in the accounts of other funerals in the diary, as for example in that of Alderman

---

[1] The present librarian of King's College states that a register of marriages in the Chapel between 1710 and 1721 is preserved in the College; but no records of those of earlier or later date are known to exist. King's College was a "peculiar," and is now in ecclesiastical view a part of the Diocese of Lincoln and not of Ely. The "peculiar" jurisdiction of the College extended over the site of the houses in front of the College abutting on what was then High Street. This probably accounts for the use of the Chapel as above.

Peddar on the 13th March, 1667, and are still more prominent in the accounts of funerals in *Machyn's Diary* before referred to. It will not be necessary to point out that it was to Matthew Wren that Pembroke College owes the building of its present Chapel under the direction of his more celebrated nephew. This is referred to in the diary. The mitre which was used in the funeral ceremony is still preserved in the College.

Dr John Pearson, by whom the funeral sermon was preached, was the future Bishop of Chester, and author of the well-known work on the Creed.

The house in which Newton resided was one of those which used to stand at the east end of St Edward's Church, as is shewn by the entry in the Corporation lease-book of the lease referred to in the diary on 16th August, 1667. These houses are shewn in Hammond's Map of the town published in 1587. The last two of their number were pulled down only a few years ago. The diarist, however, does not appear to have resided in either of these, but in one of the houses lying more to the south.

The record of the visit of the Prince of Tuscany to the University on the 1st May, 1669, contains notices of several points in the topography of the University. The mention of the Regent Walk brings to mind that the path to the Senate or Regent House, which lay to the north of the present path to the University Library, was then lined with buildings for a considerable portion of its length; and that at Trinity College the older foundation of King's Hall survived in the name "King and Queens Hostle[1]." The Comedy House belonging to the College was still standing and used for its original purpose.

At the subsequent visit of the Duchess of York on the 28th September, 1680, the Corporation received her at the house

---

[1] Three sides of the small quadrangular court of King's Hall survived till 1694, when, being ruinous, they were pulled down. The usual designation in the College Audit-Books is King's Hostel. (Willis and Clark, *Architectural History of the University and Colleges*, ii. 461.)

called New England. This was on the east side of the town, between it and the village of Barnwell, as it then was, and stood probably on some part of the present site of Maid's Causeway. It retained its name down to the end of the last century, when a lease of it was granted by the Corporation, to whom it belonged, to Mr Edward Gillam, but since that date the name disappears from the Corporation books, probably owing to its sale, of which no record was kept; nor does the locality retain any memorial of the name in its streets or lanes.

The Corporation made it their usual practice to meet their Sovereign on Christ's Pieces, as recorded on the three occasions on which the town was visited by the reigning monarch. The first of these was on the 4th October, 1671, when King Charles II. arrived in Cambridge. Newton was at that time Mayor, and Mr Pepys Recorder. He was a member of a well-known local family whose estates were at Cottenham, and a distant relative of the great diarist. The maces referred to as carried by the King's Macebearers, are still, I am informed, preserved in the royal collection, though not now carried before Her Majesty.

The members of the Corporation seem at this time to have been careful of their dignity, as they declined to greet the Ambassador from Morocco on his arrival in the town on the 1st April 1682; reserving their welcome for those "of greater quality." It seems rather strange that the Corporation should have assumed this position with regard to the Ambassador, considering that the guest of the Mayor on the occasion of the King's visit to the Borough in October 1671 was one of His Majesty's Sergeants at Mace, a gentleman of reputation no doubt, but hardly one of the highest quality. The same doubt as to the recognized position of the Corporation is aroused by the account of the reception of their representatives by the Duchess of York in September 1680. They were admitted into, and withdrew from, the Lodge of the Provost of King's College by the back door, and without their insignia, in a manner scarcely consistent with the courtesy due to the municipality.

The diarist consoles himself with the remark that the Doctors of the University went out from the Lodge in the same way, if they did not enter by it.

The single notice in the diary for the year 168⅔ is that of the fire at Newmarket, which caused the failure of the Rye House Plot, owing to the King leaving the Palace there earlier than had been originally intended. Though the fire is noticed, there is no entry relating to the plot, or its failure, though these must have been well-known facts at the time.

In fact the omissions in the diary are noticeable. Considering that the diarist was Register (as he terms it) of Trinity College from the 23rd March 167¾ down to his death in 1718, some further entries relating to his great contemporary Sir Isaac might have been expected than the meagre note of the 29th August 1689 relative to his ineligibility to hold the Provostship of King's College owing to his not being a member of that Foundation.

Many other points of interest arise on the perusal of the diary, especially the biographical ones relating to the persons mentioned, but these must be worked out in a more thorough and accessible way than is possible in this introduction.

Some of the Tavern signs mentioned in the Diary will be recognized by its readers as still existing, and attached to the same houses. These are the Red Lion in Petty Cury, its identity being shewn by its being in the parish of St Mary the Great; the Three Tuns (now turned into a Temperance hotel) situate at the corner of St Edward's Passage; and the Mitre, which stands in Bridge Street, at the corner of Blackamoor's Head Yard. The following have disappeared:—the Red *Heart* as it is called in the Diary, though it was always written *Hart* in late years, which occupied the site of Alexandra Street, known up to quite a recent period as Red Hart Yard; the celebrated Rose Tavern on the site of Rose Crescent, the back-gates of which stood a few yards distant from Trinity Street, till within the memory of some of the present residents in Cambridge; and the Dolphin, which stood at the end of

Jesus Lane, on the site now occupied by the new Hostel of Trinity College. In the same way the names of many of the residents mentioned in the diary will be familiar to the present inhabitants of Cambridge, though now borne by families represented in the neighbourhood, but not in the town itself. The following names amongst others present themselves: Finch, Bird, Muriel, Spalding, Herring, Frohock, Cropley, Bland, Crabb, and Potto. Of these only Bird, Spalding, Frohock, and Bland, seem to be now borne by actual inhabitants of the town, but Finch and Herring have only died out in recent years, whilst Muriel and Cropley are still familiar in the neighbouring city of Ely. Possibly Frohock ought now to be looked upon as belonging rather to the neighbourhood than to Cambridge itself, as families of that name have numerous members in the neighbouring villages of Cottenham, Willingham, and Over; whilst in Cambridge itself the name is scantily represented. The well-known fen name of Crabb is not apparently now extant in the Borough as a surname, though in more than one family it is borne as a second Christian name; and Potto has also died out, unless it be recognizable under the form of Potts, but it still retains its vitality in the neighbouring County of Huntingdon.

Interesting illustrations of the manners of the period are contained in various points in the diary. Attention has already been drawn to the display which seems to have been the necessary accompaniment of the funerals of the period; and of course the usual amount of feasting was necessary to carry duly on the work of the Corporation. It would be interesting to know what was the exact composition of a "sugar cake", of which such a plentiful supply seems to have been provided, from time to time, for festive or funeral occasions. The dishes actually provided seem to have been of much the same kind as those which are given at ordinary dinners now, but without the lighter dishes introduced into modern cookery by the influence of the French School. Some of the wines bear names strange to our modern ears, as for example the hypocras provided on the occasion of Mrs Wells' funeral. This was probably a sweet wine manufactured from various ingredients and corresponding to the "sack" of earlier days. Various entries in the diary shew that over-indulgence in drinking was not viewed with the same eyes as it is now, but that it was regarded as a trivial offence against society, even if it were one at all. From the description of the dinner of the 29th May, 1669, it is evident that the habit of smoking after dinner was then in fashion, though it afterwards died out, to be happily revived in modern days.

The striking example of the gross cruelty which then characterized the system of punishments authorized by law, contained in the account of the pressing to death of a prisoner at the Assizes held at Cambridge on the 7th March, 166$\frac{4}{5}$, should be noticed, especially as this form of punishment was not swept away till quite recently, viz. by the second section of the 28th chapter of the Statutes 7 and 8 Geo. IV.

This punishment supplies us with an interesting piece of legal history. In this case it will be observed that it was applied to a prisoner who would not plead. According to the ancient system of law, a prisoner who declined to plead was tortured to compel him to do so, which was, according to the terms then in force, an application of the "peine forte et dure." For the actual application of torture the punishment of pressing to death had been substituted by the time that Edward Coke wrote his work founded upon Lyttelton. The excuse for the application of this form of punishment, which seems only a more refined form of torture, was that the prisoner was considered to be "mute of malice," and therefore liable to punishment to compel him to plead. It was not until the year 1820 that a statute was passed (60 Geo. III. & 1 Geo. IV. cap. 2) to enable a plea of "not guilty" to be entered when a prisoner stood mute, thereby enabling the Judge and Jury to proceed with the trial, though the actual pressing to death was done away with in certain cases by the provisions of 12 Geo. III. c. 20, whereby the person standing mute was directed to be convicted, and thereby all difficulty was done away with, and the majesty of the law amply vindicated. The object of the prisoner's declining to plead was in many instances to avoid the forfeiture of property, and attainder of blood, which resulted from a conviction for felony. At the same Assizes at which the pressing to death was carried out it will be observed that an attorney was convicted of the offence of barratry. This crime appears now to have been removed from the Statute book, except in relation to mariners, amongst whom it means the wilful throwing away of a ship, and is one of the risks covered by a policy of marine insurance. In the case in question it appears to have meant stirring up quarrels between neighbours, which at this period seems to have been regarded with very different eyes from now.

In conclusion it should be mentioned that the author of the Diary died in the 90th year of his age, and was buried in St Edward's Church, 25 September, 1718.

.... Newton of Newcastle in Co: Northumb.

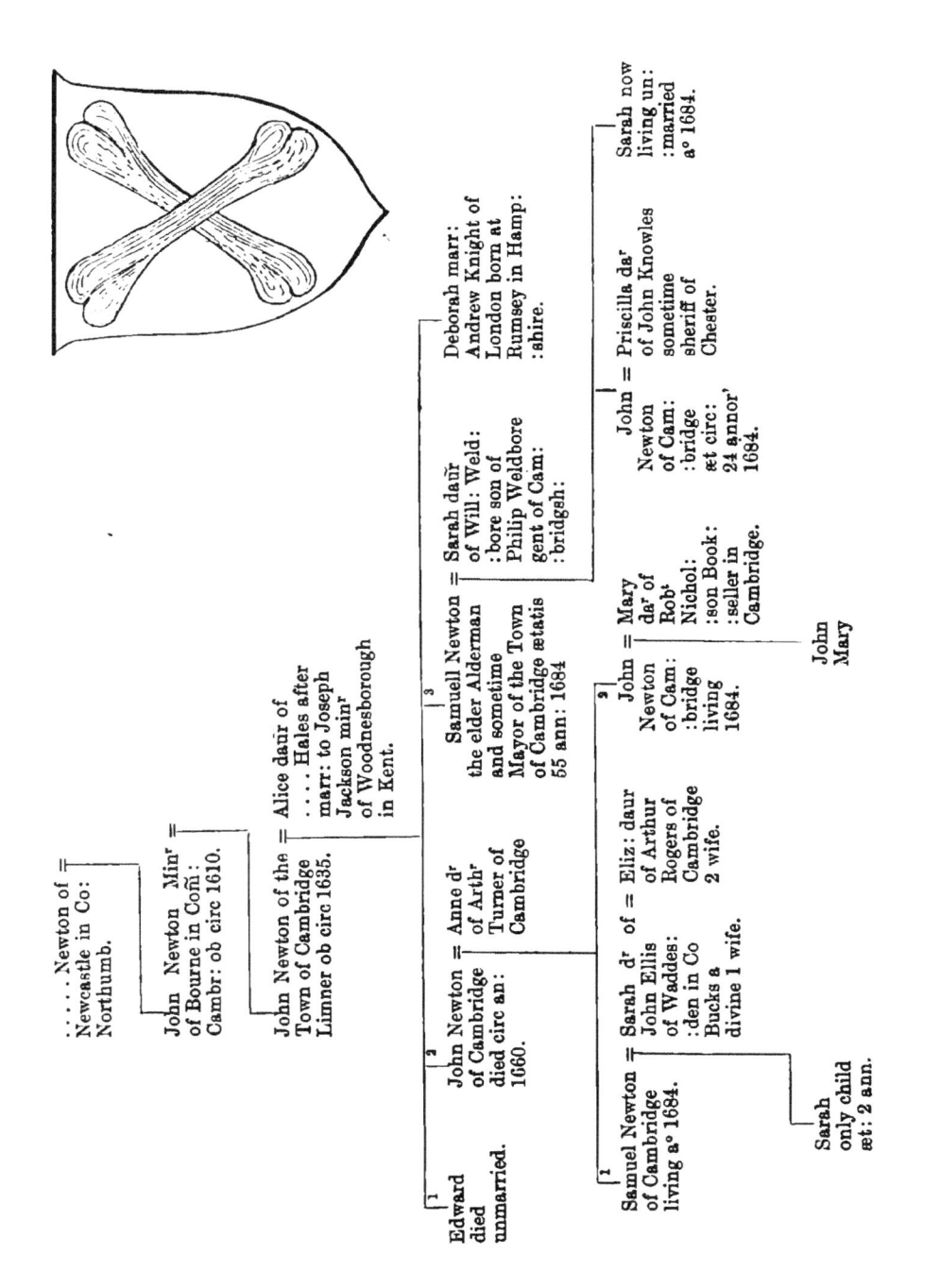

John Newton Minr of Bourne in Com̃: Cambr: ob circ 1610. ==

John Newton of the Town of Cambridge Limner ob circ 1635. == Alice daũr of .... Hales after marr: to Joseph Jackson minr of Woodnesborough in Kent.

1	2	3
Edward died unmarried.	John Newton of Cambridge died circ an: 1660. == Anne dr of Arthr Turner of Cambridge.	Samuell Newton the elder Alderman and sometime Mayor of the Town of Cambridge ætatis 55 ann: 1684 == Sarah daũr of Will: Weld: bore son of Philip Weldbore gent of Cam: :bridgsh:

Deborah marr: Andrew Knight of London born at Rumsey in Hamp: :shire.

1	2	3
Samuel Newton of Cambridge living aº 1684. == Sarah dr of John Ellis of Wadded:den in Co Bucks & divine 1 wife. = Eliz: daur of Arthur Rogers of Cambridge 2 wife.	John Newton of Cam: :bridge living 1684. == Mary dar of Robt Nichol: :son Book: :seller in Cambridge.	John Newton of Cam: :bridge ætat circ: 24 annor' 1684. = Priscilla dar of John Knowles sometime sheriff of Chester.

Sarah only child æt: 2 ann.

John Mary

Sarah now living un: :married aº 1684.

THE DIARY OF SAMUEL NEWTON. [1660

On Fryday the 11th May 1660 King Charles the Second was proclaymed King by John Ewin Chandler then Maior of Cambridge. The Maior himselfe read the Proclamacion, the Towne Clerke more audibly spoke it after him;

With the Maior, was the Recorder in his Gowne, and all the Aldermen in their Scarlet Gownes on horseback, and all the freemen on horseback. They proclaimed twice (in 2 severall places) in the great Markett Place

> once on the Pease hill
> and against St Buttolphs Church
> and beyound the Great Bridge
> and against Jesus Lane
> and against Trinity Church

In all these places was Hee proclaymed, at night many bonfires in Towne, 4 on the great Market Hill. great expressions and acclamacions of Joy from all sorts.

On Thirsday the 10th of May 1660 it was the King was proclaymed by the University about 3 of the clock in the afternoone, 1ª on the Crosse in the great Market place, and then in the middle of the Market place against the Rose.

On Saturday the 12th May 1660 the King was proclaymed at Kings College; all the souldiers were placed round on the topp of their chappell from whence they gave a volley of shott.

(The entries so far were made on a loose sheet of paper, which was afterwards folded up and carried about and eventually fastened into the book. The next entry was probably copied in then.)

1660

Vppon Tewsday the 8th day of January Anno Domini 1660 *at a Common day I Samuel Newton was made Free Burgesse of the Corporacion of Cambridge, Mr Edward Chapman being then Mayor, Thomas Brand, John Cooper, John Bird, and Ralph Rule being then Bayliffs, Mr Thomas Muryell and Mr Nathaniel Crabb being then Threasurers; my freedome there cost me 6ˡⁱ: 5ˢ: 1ᵈ vizt for my fine 5ˡⁱ the fees of the house 15ˢ 1ᵈ and given to the Serjeants 10ˢ and at the same day was my sister Ellis and my wife both being present admitted to 5 boothes in Stirbridge fayre, the same day was my brother Ellis made free, our freedome being first granted us and wee seuerally sworne, before the admission of our wives.*

1664

On the   day of   Anno Domini 1664 Samuel Newton and Thomas Mace were elected Treasurers for the Towne of Cambridge for the yeare commenceing from Michaelmas 1664.

1664
Septʳ. 28

I, and Mʳ Mace, at Mʳ Towne Clerkes house sealed 2 bonds to the Towne, each bond being 500ˡⁱ wherein wee were bound the one for the other, the condicions of the said bonds were for the true discharge of our Office, and the Accounts depending thereuppon: each of us paid for our bond to the Towneclerke 1ˢ.

Septemb: 29

Mʳ Mace and I, were this day at a Common day before dinner sworne for the discharge of our office. At the same Common day, and in the first place was sworne Francis Finch confeccioner Mayor of Cambridge for the said yeare, after him, then were sworne the 4 Bayliffes of the said Towne for the said yeare vizt John Adams carpenter Bayliffe of the Bridge Ward,   Jennings Inholder Bayliffe of the Talbooth, Peter Lightfoot fishmonger Bayliffe of Reach fayre Liberty, and Samuel Richardson Milliner Bayliffe O: then were sworne the Coroners for the said yeare vizt.

Attorney at Law and Tho: Fox Inholder one of the 24^{ty} and last of all we the Treasurers were sworne; At the same day was Nathaniel Crabb, Skinner elected to be Alderman of the said Towne, in the roome and place of Christopher Rose then lately deceased, who some few dayes after in manner usuall, declared or signified his acceptacion thereof; On this Michaelmas day according to our instruccions, wee the new Treasurers about 8 in the morning went to Mr New Elects, where came the Recorder and severall of the Aldermen and some of the Bayliffs, where wee had sugar cakes and wine, from thence the Newelect and the rest, went to the Old Mayors (Mr Clench) where wee had nothing; after the company came there together all went from thence to Trinity Church, everyone in his order the Mayor and New Elect first &c. one Mr Cogey of Pembroke Hall preached on this Text *Feare God and honour the King* *Prov. By mee Kings reigne and Princes decree Justice.* After sermon the whole company went to the Towne Hall everyone in order two and two, and first the Threasurers, that new came in, then every one according to his place and seniority. When the new Treasurers came to the Hall staire foot doore, there they stood, untill the Attorneyes first and then the Mayor &c. followeing went upp into the Hall; after Common day was done, dinner being prepared wee went to it. *The new Maior and old Maior sitt at the upper end, onely the new Maior has the upper hand*, it seemes the manner is for the new Treasurers to sitt at the 24^{ty} mans table, Mr Mace did, but I was placed at the Aldermans table, where besides the Aldermen sate the Attorneyes and strangers. After dinner the New Mayor, Old Mayor, Recorder, Aldermen, 24^{ty}, Bayliffs, Treasurers, Attorneyes and as many of the ffreemen as pleased went home with the New Mayor to his house, where wee had sugar cakes clarrett white and sack of each one cupp every man, afterwards every man departed at his pleasure, I did not perceive the Old Mayor was attended home by any;

Nath. Crabb chose Alderman

* M^r Fr. Finch Mayor

October 2 : Sunday, the 4 New Bayliffes and new Treasurers waited on Mr Mayor to Church, and home againe, wee all dyned there this day.

Oct: 1 Saturday being the next Saturday after Michaellmasse day wee the Threasurers according to custome, collected of every person haueing a fish stall and of every person haueing a butchers stall or standing in the markett for every stall or standing an acknowledge 1^d and the like did the Bayliffe of the Talbooth to whome it did belong, to our assistance wee had 2 Serjeants vizt Tim: Marsh and Tho: Harper, to whome for their attendance we gave 12^d a peice, wee the Treasurers for our parts gathered by the said pense then 9^s 3^d whereof wee spent 9^d at Tim: Marshes, and gave 12^d a peice to the Serjeants and soe had cleere to our selves 3^s 3^d a peice.

Octob: 21th Fryday, in the morning betweene 9 and 10 met at Great St Maryes Church the Mayor and Vice Chauncellor, before whome then met and were empannelled the paveing Leet, Robert Ridgewell Inholder being sworne the foreman of that Jury, the Bayliffes were there with Mr Mayor but not the Treasurers. The new Treasurers are to gather upp the amerciaments of this Leet for the defaults in paveing *and have but 6 weekes time after Michaelmas to gather them, yet upon any deniall after demand thereof, the Treasurers entring an accion at the Towne suit, may prosecute at leisure.*

October 22th
The Vice Chancellor with the rest of that body makes proclamacion yearely for the selling of wholsome fish victuall &c.

Saturday, in the morning about 10 of the clock D^{or} Fleetwood then Vice Chancellor, with the Proctors Taxers and some Doctors, as the custome yearely is, (the University being Clerkes of the Markett,) made proclamacion thrice, and caused to be proclaimed the orders and penaltyes concerninge the selling of fish, victuall &c. *these proclamacions are made in each Markett place.*

Oct: 25th Tewsday (being Court day), Court and Leet was then holden at the Guildhall from 8 to 10 in the morning, where after the busines of the Court was ended, were sworne the

Leet of Annoyances (Jennings Chandler being the foreman of that Inquest,) they were appointed to deliver in their Verdict on this day fortnight to which day the Court was adiorned, afterwards were sworne the 5 pounders to make their true presentments to the said Inquest. Noat that at all Court dayes there is paid for every cause by the Attorney for the same; 6^d: vizt to the hands of the Treasurers for the pore mans box 2^d; and iiii^d to the sergeants amongst them, which they put in to a box and devide betweene themselves. this day was received by the Treasurers for the poore mans box for 21 causes 3^s 6^d.

Wednesday; I received the verdict of the Paving Leet from Robert Ridgwell that brought it mee hee being the foreman of that Inquest, to which verdict (being in a long roll of paper) the hands as well of the Vniuersity Jury as of the Towne Jury were sett and not their seales: I paid then unto Robert Ridgwell aforesaid for the said verdict 17^s; vizt 6^s for the foreman and 11^s for the other 11 of that Inquest, which verdict I immediately retourned to the Towne Clerke to be transcribed, and for a warrant to be thereupon made, for gathering the amerciaments.   Oct 26

Tewsday, haueing received from Mr Towne Clarke the Estreat and amerciaments Mr Mace and I went to Mr Mayor to have the warrant for collecting the same sealed, who accordingly sealed the same, with the seale wherewith execucions are sealed; the same day wee went to gather upp the amerciaments taking to our assistance Tim. Marsh sergeant, at whose house before our goeing out I and Mr Mace spent 6^d a peice.   Nov: 1st

Thirsday, Mr Mace and my selfe and the said sergeant went to make an end in gathering the said amerciaments wee went to all that were amerced but some not being within, afterwards came and discharged the same or gaue us satisfaccion.   Nov. 3

Sunday. being the first Sunday after Hollowmas and the first Sunday of the month was the Obijt sermon of John Fan late Alderman of Cambr' who by his will gaue unto   Nov: 6

the Mayor Bayliffes and Burgesses of Cambr' 2 boothes in Stirbridge fayre on condicion that the maior with 3 of the senior of the Aldermen assistant to him should disburse 4ˡⁱ vizt 10ˢ to the poore, 10ˢ to the minister that preaches that sermon, and the rest to charitable uses, of which the Bayliffs haue 8ᵈ a peice, the Treasurers that pay the obijt money there present haue 6ᵈ a peice. At this Obijt collacion (wᶜʰ at the hall was a sugar cake and one cup of sack to euery one) were present the Mayor Aldermen Bayliffes and myselfe as Treasurer and as many of the 24ᵗʸ as pleased. Mʳ Peachill fellow of Magdalen Coll: preached this sermon at Great Sᵗ Maryes, his Text was the 2 Rom. part of the 14 verse, Are a Law to themselves. The old Treasurers are at the Hall then present (without their gownes) to pay the said Obijt money. The Bayliffes and Treasurers dyned this day at Mʳ Mayors, onely were absent Mʳ Mace and Peter Lightfoot.

John Fanns Obijt

Sunday being the second Sunday after Hallomasse was Alderman *Foxton* * Chevin his * Obijt sermon, I was not at it; the sermon was at Great Sᵗ Maryes.

*Nov 13 Alderm. * Chevins obijt* Foxton's Obiit*

Tewsday, Griffith Finch, was marryed at Great St Maryes Church in Cambr' to Mary Williamson spinster who was daughter to his fathers wife.

Nov 22 Gr. Finch mar.

Saturday I paid Mr Towne Clerke for the coppy of the estreat of and warrant for the amerciaments 10ˢ.

Dec. 4.

Tewsday I and Mʳ Mace accounted about the amerciaments, and wee found wee had collected 3ˡⁱ : 10ˢ : 0ᵈ : Of this wee paid out to the Jury that made the amerciaments 17ˢ and to the Towne Clerke 10ˢ and in regard wee had noe supper at the house of the Serjeant (wᶜʰ was Tim: Marsh) that went along with us, wee gaue him for his two dayes paines 10ˢ soe that besides all expences wee had to our selves cleere 16ˢ a peice.

Dec 7

Wednesday, this night I supped at Alderman Crabbs, where alsoe then supped the Aldermen, Bayliffs and Treasurers *but none of their wives*. Mʳ Mayor was then at

Dec 14

London, the Serjeants invited the guests: noe woman supped with the company but Mrs Crabb; *Mr Chapman at this time Dep. Maior.*

Saturday: in the morning betimes dyed Roger Nightingale Manciple or Caterer and singing man of Kings College; some say he dyed on the night before being fryday night. {Dec 17}

(An entry which follows has been carefully obliterated.)

The same day in the morning from about 2 of the clock to 5 was seene in the ayre a Comett wch seueral dayes lately before had bin alsoe seene, the star it selfe was very little or not at all bigger then an ordinary starr, but it had a ray wch came from it that appeared to the judgem^t. of some to be 20 yards in length, to others the length of a pyke, to others the length of Kings Coll Chappell, it appeared southeastward. {A Comett seene}

Tewsday Court day. here was 2 tryalls or verdicts, and after Court was adiorned, the poore mans box was opened, wherein was found about 11^s wch the mayor at his pleasure distributed, vizt to 4 poore prisoners in the Talbooth 6^s, to the 6 spittle poore 3^s, to Mrs Wickham 18^d &c. {Dec 20. Poore mans box distributed.}

Wednesday. I paid the Towne waytes there yeares wages 3^li the same day I rec^d the rent booke from the Towne Clerke. {Dec 21}

Saturday being X^tmas Eve Mr Mace and I as Treasurers sent in to Mr Mayor, by ourselues, a Cagg of Sturgeon wch cost of Mr Wells 16^s. wee sent it in about 10 of the clock this morning, the Bayliffs sent in their presents this day alsoe by themselues. {Dec 24}

Sunday, being X^tmas day, as the custome is, the Bayliffs and Treasurers are absent from Mr Mayor this day; This day according to Custome the serjeants and Gaoler and their wives dine at Mr Mayors. {Dec 25}

Fryday wee the Treasurers and our wiues as alsoe all the Aldermen, Bayliffs, and Attorneyes and Towne Clerke and their wives were invited to dine with Mr Mayor on Tewsday following. {Dec 30}

Dec 31	Saturday, seuerall of the Aldermen sent in presents to Mr Mayor as namely Ald'. Simpson 2 turkeys, 2 capons, and 2 couple of wildefoule, Crabb 2 capons, 2 rabbetts 2 couple of wildefoule &c.

166$\frac{4}{5}$.

Jan 1	Sunday being new yeares day and the first Sunday in the month the Bayliffes and Treasurers dyned at Mr Mayors.
Jan 3	Tewsday I and Mr Mace alsoe the Recorder Aldermen Bayliffs Attorneyes Towne Clerke and wiues according to Frydayes Invitacion dined at Mr Mayors, seuerall of us supped there alsoe the same night.
Jan 5	Thursday. This morning being a great frost, Mr Greswold ma{r} of Arts and Fellow of Trinity Coll in Cambr' fell downe the stayres wch are next the chappell north by the Kings gate, and with the fall was killed, being found dead there lyeing, (about 5 in the morning by the bedmakers) and
Mr Greswold killed by a fall downe Tr Coll stayres	was cold and stiff, he had the key of the garden dore in his hand and lay with his head downwards at the feet of the stayres and his heels upwards upon the stayres, with his neck (as was supposed) choked with his high coller, some bloud had come out of his nose, being seene on his band, Humfry Prychard the Coll porter lett him into the Coll about 2 of the clock that morning and was supposed to have bin drinking somewhere, and haueing bin as was supposed through the garden at the house of easement at his retourne goeing up the said stayres to his chamber fell downe and was killed as aforesaid.
Jan 11 Mrs Wells dyed	Wednesday betweene 5 and 6 at night dyed Mrs Susanna Wells the wife Alderman Wm Wells at the 3 Tunns. Shee lay sick about one weeke.
Jan: 15.	Sunday Mrs Wells was buryed in the great chancell at G{t} St Maryes in Cambr' at the upper end higher then Do{r} Butlers monum{t}, Mr Hill of Trinity Coll (not the red hayred man) preached her funerall sermon, his text was on these words (man continueth not in honor but is like the beast that perish). There was a great funerall but little solemnity, many people

but small order, the Colledges served in their Colledge Halls, and the rest of the Towne at the 3 Tunns and some other houses neere Shee was borne by M͡r of Arts, noe gloues nor ribbons, seruice one cup of claret, one cup of Ipocras... sugar cakes, 2 roles and the [b]est sort onely 2 mackeroons.

Sunday before Candlemasse day was an obijt sermon being M͡r Chevins this the old Treasurers and is the last of the obijts they provide and pay for. *Jan 29 M͡r Chevins Obijt sermon*

Munday came to Trinity Coll. L͡d Keeling, Judge of Assize, (there being him onely that came that Circuit) he came from Bury assizes, and was heere betweene 4 and 5 in the afternoone, Cambridge Assizes was on Tewsday the day following: soe soone as wee had informacion by one of the Towne Serjeants, that the Judge his Steward was come in (for he comes in a little while before the Judge) M͡r Mace and I together with 2 Towne Serjeants Thom: Harper and Jo: Bridge, went along with the butcher and fishmonger with the Towne present to Trinity Coll. Kitchin where wee taryed a little while, and then came the Judge his Steward, to whome I went with M͡r Mace and tould him that M͡r Maior and the Aldermen of the Towne presented their service to the Judge and had sent him a present, the particulers of w͡ch present wee deliuered to the Steward in writing, w͡ch were, one Veale, one Sheepe, one Pyke, two Duches, two Eales, and six perches, the veale was prized to us by the butcher at xl͡s and the sheepe at xxv͡s. The pyke was prized to us by Turkey at 16͡s: the 2 Duches 6͡s the 2 eles 6͡s and the perches   , after our message done to the Steward wee tooke our leaues and came away, he tould us he would acquaint his Lord͡pp with the present: and desired of us to know who were the Towne officers that attended us, wee tould him the 2 Serjeants there, to whome he said there was somewhat by him to be giuen for their attendance. At the Judges comeing in to the Court, The Master and some of the Seniors mett him to complement him, soone after his comeing to the Lodgeing, came the Vice Chaunceller &c. They presented the Judge with a pair of imbroydered gloues *March 6 Lent Assizes* between 20 and 30ˢ price, after their visitt went the Maior Recorder and Alderman to complement him.

March: 7 — Tewesday was the Assizes held at the Castle of Cambr' the same day (among others) was at the bar arraigned *for robbery of one Mʳ Morden* one who named himself Perrey, Execucion (but it was *then thought to be* Edward Sterne *as after appeared* *that was apprentice to my brother Welbore*) (*yet I think he denyed it*) he would not plead but stood mute wherefore the Judge gaue sentence he should be pressed to death presently, wᶜʰ accordingly the same day was done *betweene 5 and 7 in the afternoone, he was about an houre a dyeing* at his pressing he confest himselfe guilty of the robbery and of many other robberyes.

March 9 — Thirsday was condemned *at the same Assizes* Nelson sonne of Roger Nelson of ffoxton for cutting the throat and murdering his wife, The same day was Roger Peapys Esqʳᵉ Recorder of Cambr' bound ouer by Recognizance to his good behaviour, for speaking words slightly of my Lᵈ Cheife Justice Hide, wᶜʰ words was sworne agˢᵗ Mʳ Peapys by Dᵒʳ Eade occasioned upon Dʳ Eades needles complaint *at the Sessions* about his being ouer rated to the poore; and the words as Dʳ Eade swore were spoke by the Recorder at the Sessions before the assizes.

Patteson — *Saturday John Patteson an Attorney at Law stood in the Pillory on the Pease hill in Cambr': from about a quarter after 11 in the forenoone, to about halfe an houre after 12 of the clock haueing fastned to the fore part of his hat being* March 11 *on his head a paper written in capitall letters (a common Barrettor) being sentenced by Judge Keeling at the said Assizes on Wednesday the 8 March 1664 to the said punishment for Barretry.*

March 11 — Saturday, was the said Nelson (together with Execution another man for stealing a mare) hanged at the place usuall for execucion in Cambr' Castle betweene 9 and 10 in the morning.

March 16: Thursday was the Auditt for the Towne of Cambr' at the Guildhall of the same Towne, Auditors were Alderman Ewin, Alderm: Chapman, Alderm: Herring, Alderm: Simpson Owen Mayfield, Phillip Williams, Sam: Moodey, / Mr Law Towne Clerk took the acc^t, it appeared uppon the foote of the acc^t that there was due to Mr Felstead baker and Mr Townesend Threasurers for that yeare 34^{li} od money, wee the new Treasurers were invited thither by the old, and all of us, Aldermen, 24^{ty} and Treasurers new and old in our gownes, they went to their accounts betweene 8 and 9 in the morning, There was a very good dinner, wch came to 4^{li} 7^s or thereabouts, besides the Auditors and Towne Clerke and Treasurers new and old were *present* at dinner Mr Mayor Mr Alderm: Wells, and some of the 24^{ty} were invited but came not. Towne Auditt

Thirsday Mr Mayor Mr Recorder the Aldermen as many as pleased and soe of the 24^{ty} went on fishing according to custome, they had 3 boates with netts, they drew Neuncham pitt, Cambr'. mills pitt and soe fisht downe to Bullen where wee had our fish drest, the charge of this—for wine bread and cheese in the boate and after at Bullen, together with boate hire came to 5^{li} od money, the mace did not goe with the Mayor *none were* in gownes, The mayor and Aldermen invited with them the Vice Chancellor *then D^{or} Sparroue*, but he went not, also D^{or} Fleetewood, D^{or} Dillingham and D^{or} Stoyl who went and dyned with them at Bullen. March 23

Fishing

Counsellors from Michaelmas 1664 For the Corporacion of the Towne of Cambr' 2 of wch are allwayes to allow of and signe all bills that the Treasurers payes unlesse it bee by order made at a Common day. Mr Ewin
Mr Herring
Mr Mayfeild
Mr Bloefeild

1665.

Sunday being Easterday, none of the Bayliffs nor Treasurers doe attend Mr Maior that day in the morning, they may if they will in the afternoone. this day all the Serjeants and their wives dine there. March 26

Wednesday was a fast appointed by his Matie in refference to the Dutch Warr and kept. Apr 5

Apr 6	Thirsday There was a presse heere in Towne for Souldiers in his Ma^tles service against the Dutch, there were prest out of Cambr'. betweene 3 and 4 score, of wch number was John Sparkes the sonne of Mr John Sparkes baker, who this day, went from Cambr'. to the rest of the souldiers who were gone before this day towards Harrage *where* at *which* *this* Time lay our ffleete consisting of about 190 and odd shipps, the number of men that man'd them was about 25000, great guns about 4600.
Souldiers prest	
1665 Aprill 3 Commett	Munday This morning at three of the clock I arose and went to the hogg hill where I plainly beheld the commett, wch appeared very low in the firmament full east with the streame or ray wch darted upwards westward, the streame to seeme was 2 or 3 yards long, and the starre and streame was much like the former that lately appeared, onely this was somewhat bigger, and the streame of this somewhat longer.
March 9— Bagly dyed	Sunday, this morning dyed Mr Bagley Minister or curate of Barnewell, and St Peters, and one of the Conducts of Kings Colledge.
March 11 Hock Tewsday New Treasurers	Tewsday, being Hock Tewsday was a grand Common day for the Towne of Cambr'. chosen then for Treasurers for the ensueing yeare Nicholas West hatter, and John More Chairemaker, severall others were then first chosen but fined for it.
May 1— Reach fayre	Munday being the day after Rogacion Sunday, was Reach fayre day, whereunto went Mr Finch Mayor and 2 or 3 of the Aldermen, the Treasurers uses to attend on the Mayor, but I was not there, there was 4 red coates in their coates there and the cryer with his new coat being provided by the Treasurers.
May 29 King's birthday	Munday being the King's birthday
June 3 Great guns at sea heard at Cambr:	Saturday all day long was heard the noyse of gunns in the ayre and I myselfe heard the noyse of them betweene 4 and 6 in the afternoone and againe betweene 9 and 10 the same night, it was generally thought heere at Cambr': that

the English and Dutch were at the same time engaged in fight.

August— being common day was elected Rowland Simpson draper Alderman, for Maior for the ensueing yeare, and for Bayliffes, Jennings Bayliffe of the bridge: Peter New Elect Lightfoot Bayliffe of the Talbooth, Samuel Richardson Bayliffe of Reach fayre, and Towensend baker Bayliffe O. (he being one of the Treasurers in 1665 the yeare when I came on) at wch time Mr Simpson took the oath proper to the New elect and whereas the New elect uses to giue a treatment at his house to the Company after Common day ended, in regard of the Infeccion then in Towne and danger thereof, it was thought fitt by him and accordingly he did giue wine and cakes at the hall vizt. all Gownemen each had a glasse or 2 of sack and 2 sugar cakes, the rest of the freemen had alsoe wine and cakes. Peter Lightfoote new Bayliffe of the Talbooth from the Hall invited as many as he pleased to drink wine to the Rose Tauern vizt. all the electors, new and old bayliffes and Treasurers Towne Clerk Attorneyes and spent on them there about 40^s.

Munday it pleased God that Jennings the August Bayliffe dyed, as was feared of the sicknes but assuredly of A Towne a vyolent feuuer that distracted him, he sickned the fryday dyed before.

Thirsday Bartholm. Day, it was conceived necessary to Aug 24 elect a Bayliffe in the roome of Jennings, and accordingly the same Electors that last before had chosen the maior and Bayliffes, chose Robt. Fuller Chandler to be Bayliffe in his roome *vizt. Bayliffe of the Talbooth till Michaelmas,* and the Common day was adjorned till the Tewsday following *when* *at which time* the said Fuller was to give in his direct answer, at wch time at first he peremptorily refused and denyed to hold, whereupon the Recorder tould him he did that w^ch *neither* became him nor any true subject of the A New K^gs for it was an afront to the King to decline his service Bayliffe elected. being thereto legally elected although he was sure to be a loser thereby and was to be blamed that he would not trust to the Courtesy of the Corporacion *not* to see him a looser in his place, and therefore ordered the Towne Clerke to sett downe 10ˡⁱ for his fine for refusing and alsoe that an informacion should be made ag⁵ᵗ him in the Exchequer and prosecuted hereupon and by advice of friendes Fuller accepted of the Bayliwick and was sworne and took his place with the Bayliffs, and by the Electors aforesaid was alsoe afterwards the same Common day elected Bayliffe of the Bridge for the ensueing yeare.

It pleased God at this Season, the Plague was very rageing and greatly encreasing in London, soe that the bill of mortality of London from the 15 August to the 22ᵗʰ 1665 was thus viz⁴.

<small>Great Plague in London</small>

Buryed within the walls 538, whereof of the Plague	366
Buryed in the 16 parishes without the walls of the Plague	2139
Buryed in the 12 out parishes in Middlesex and Surrey of the Plague	1244
Buryed in the 5 parishes of the Citty and libertyes of Westmʳ. of the Plague	483
Christned this weeke in toto	171
Buryed this weeke Males . . 2777	
Females . 2791	
In all	5568
whereof of the Plague	4237

Increased in the buryalls this weeke 249 Parishes cleere 27, infected 103.

The parish which in this weeke was most infected was Sᵗ Giles Cripplegate where dyed this weeke 847 whereof of the Plague 572.

And in the Bill of Mortality of London from the 22 August to the 29ᵗʰ 1665 it was thus viz⁴.

<small>Still a greater Plague in London wʰ God in much mercy abate.</small>

Buryed in the 97 parishes within the walls 933, whereof of the Plague	700
Buryed in the 16 parishes without the walls 3627 whereof of the Plague	2928

Buryed in the 12 out parishes of Middlesex and
   Surrey 2045, whereof of the Plague . . 1759
Buryed in the 5 parishes of the Citty and libertyes
   of Westm^r 891, whereof of the Plague . . 715

Christned this weeke in toto 169
Buryed in all 7496
   whereof of the Plague 6102.

Increased in the Buryalls this weeke 1928. parishes cleere 17 infected 113. The parish wherein, in this weeke the most dyed was St Giles Cripplegate, where then dyed in toto 842, whereof of the plague 605.

Saturday was then posted up in Cambr' the Kings Proclamacion, that Sturbridge fayre should not this yeare be kept because of the great Plague at London thereby prohibiting all Londoners from comeing to the same, Great Danger was alsoe then heere in Cambr' seuerall dyeing then heere in Cambr' and at the pesthouses of the sicknes.

Sept 1

(The rest of the page is left blank.)

The plague increased still untill Oct. 1665

166$\frac{5}{6}$.

Wednesday being Fast day, John Jacklyn the head Towne Serjeant dyed, about 3 of the clock in the afternoone.

Jan: 3.

1666.

On Sunday betweene one and 2 of the clock in the morning the Citty of London began in Pudding Lane there at a french bakers house to be fyred (and it being a great north-east winde) continued most feircely burneing from that time untill Thirsday in the afternoone following being the 6th day of the same September. it burned down   parishes with the Churches and consumed all along from where it began, to the Tower, and *alsoe* towards Westminster as far as Temple Barr. not aboue 2 or 3 persons that were consumed by the fire, and for light commodityes and wch were of most

2 September 1666
London fyred.

value, most persons got them away into the fields, but at such vast rates for carriage that 8 or 10^{li} for the carriage of a load of goodes was ordinarily giuen.

I haue read that formerly in the time and Reigne of King Etheldred who was buryed in St Paules, great part of the Citty was destroyed by fire.

Octob. 13: Heavens seemed to be on fire — being Saturday from 5 to about halfe an houre after 6 at night the northwest part of the heavens (in my thoughts) seemed many times to burne and bee all of a redd fire, it came after the manner of lightning but the flashes much more red (even as fire) alsoe much more large and of longer continuance, there was alsoe 2 small thunderclapps or rumblings in the ayre. This and with a Tempest that in accompanyed did overturne many houses and the greatest part of a Church.

Octob. 26. On Fryday I and my wife and family came from Waterbeach to Cambr'. wee haueing been in the Countrey there in regard of the sicknes in Cambr'. ever since Saturday the 23 June 1666.

Novembr. 1. On *Fryday* Thirsday dyed Peter Thurloes wife at the hand of the sicknesse.

Nov. 2. On Fryday at night about 11 of the clock Mr James Valentine goeing out of his chamber downe the Stayres into Trinity Colledge Court, gott such a fall that for a good space he lay as dead and bruised and cutt his head and blead much, and its feared much that he will not recouer it.*

Nov. 3. Saturday its said in Cambr'. that this day London was againe on fire, and began at a Brewers house in .

Nov. 5. Munday, my mayd Frances Preston went from mee, and the same day came to me my mayd Anne Beecham.

Nov. 20: Mr Wells marryed to Mrs Allen. — Tewsday: Wm Wells Vintner one of the Aldermen of Cambridge was marryed vnto Jane Allen widdow the Relict of Richard Allen Vintner late one of the Aldermen of the same Towne (at K^{gs} Coll: Chappell).

* Mr Valentine dyed of this hurt on *Wednesday* Thirsday morning being the 9th Nov. 1666.

On Sunday Morning dyed Thomas Browne Clerke of great St Maryes in Cambr': and was buryed on the same Sunday night. *Decemb. 2 Browne St Maryes Clerke dyed.*

On Munday in the afternoone at a meeting of the parishioners at Great St Maryes Church, was John Aungier draper with a full consent chosen (in the roome of Browne deceased) Clerke of Great St Maryes in Cambr': he performed his duty and Office the same night at the buryall of   Miller sonne of Edward Miller at the Red Lyon, being the first buryall he had in his said place. *Decemb: 3 Aungier chosen Clerke of St Maryes.*

[166⁵⁄₇]

On Tewsday was the first time John Newton my sonne went to the Grammer Free Schoole in Cambridge. *Feb: 12th*

On Tewsday D^{or} Robt Brady Ma^r of Caijus Coll: gaue mee his order under his hand to Mr Griffith Ma^r of the said schoole for his receiving the said John Newton in the same schoole. *Feb: 26: Jo. Newton entred by Dr Bradyes order into the Free schoole.*

On Thursday in the morning betweene 9 and 10 of the clock at the Assizes holden for the County of Cambr', and in respect of the then very cold season kept in the Towne of Cambr': for life and death at the Towne Hall where sat Judge Wyndham, and for the Nisi Prius, next the Towne Hall in the Buthery or Buttermarkett in a place there boarded satt Judge Morton, before whome was then and there tryed the cause betweene Mr John Byng of Grancester and Thomas Terry of Cambr': brought by Mr Byng agst Terry upon the Statute of forgery; and the verdict of the Jury was agst Terry for forgery of a writt against Mr Bing whereupon Terry *had* caused the said Mr Byng to be arrested and imprisoned in the Castell; *and further the Jury gaue to Mr Byng agst Terry damage to* 300^{li}. *March 7th: Tho: Terry an Attorney convict of forgery*

C. A. S. Octavo Series. XXIII.

March 8th
Sr Charles
Wheeler
chosen a
Vniversity
Burgesse

On Fryday at the Regent House of the Vniversity of Cambr' was in the place of S.r Thomas Fanshaw deceased elected and chose S.r Charles Wheeler to be one of the Burgesses for the said Vniversity to sitt in Parliament.

1667.

Bpp of Ely dyed

On or about Wednesday the 24 April 1667 dyed at Ely house in London, Matthew Wrenn Lord Bishopp of Ely.

May 9th

On Thirsday in the afternoone about 6 of the clock was brought to Cambr. the body of Matthew Wrenn Lord Bishopp of Ely in a herse Coach hung round with his Escocheons, it being drawne with 6 horses, a postillion riding on one of the forehorses, when he was brought through Trumpington the Bell there tolled, when through little S.t Maryes the bell rang out there, when through S.t Buttolphs the bell there tolled and soe did at Bennett when he was brought through there but S.t Edwards Bell stirred not, Great S.t Maryes Bell rang out a great while. There came along with the herse Coach, 4 other coaches in mourning, each coach haueing 6 horses as I take it, and about half a dozen horsemen in mourning, and about a dozen other parsons and gentlemen came along with the coach.

B.ph of Elyes funeral solemnity

From the time of the said Bishopps comeing in as before is mencioned, hee being carryed into the Schooles of this Vniversity, and sett in a little roome there darkned and hung in all parts with black cloath, (it being the roome *at the lower end* as you goe into the lower schooles w.ch is under the Regent House) the said Bishopp from that time till his funerall solempnization lay in state after this manner, The corps being in lead and in a large Coffin was about 3 foot high from the ground over the Corps or Herse to the ground lay a black velvett herse cloath w.ch at the bottome (for about an inch *wide*) was edged round about with white sarcenet, over the midst of the Herse was spread the coat of the King or Herald at Armes, having the Kings Armes on crimson sattin, ritchly embroidered with gold, at the head of the

Hearse was standing the Bishops Miter wch was *either beaten gold or* silver guilt, the capp *or inpart* whereof was crimson sattin or silk, the Miter was plaine saving some little flower wrought on the middle on each side thereof and on the topp of each side a little crosse of about an inch in length and breadth. On the one side of the top of the hearse lay along the Bishopps Crosier of silver *somewhat* in likeness to a Sheapherds Crooke, of about an ell long, and in thicknes round about 2 inches and a halfe. the floore of the roome was covered either with black cloath or bayes or els was matted; on each side of the herse stood 3 wax tapers in Candlesticks, and on each side of the herse attended 2 poore schollers in mourning gownes bare, vizt 2 on each side the head and 2 on each side the feete, all persons that came in to see, stood bare there, all that desired might see, none denyed neither poor nor *rich* ritch, Towne nor Country and without anything to be given or taken. From hence

On the 11th May being Saturday *betweene* 3 *and* *about* 4 of the Clock in the afternoone, the schoole Bell in Great St Maryes therefore ringing out was the Bishopp borne by 6 ordinary persons in course gownes (whereof Corn: Austin the joyner was one, Philips a laborer of Trin: Coll: another Bradley a freemason another &c.) for the solempnity of his funerall from the schooles to Pembroke Hall *it was* in this manner vizt:

May 11.

1. First went 2 old men in course mourning gownes by name Wilson the taylor Clerke of little St Maryes, and Billops the joyner with sticks in their hands sutable.

2. After them followed 28 poore schollers (*in order two and two*) in mourning gownes for that service appointed whereof 7 were of Pembroke Hall, 7 of Peterhouse, 7 of Jesus Colledge and 7 of St Johns Colledge.

3. After them followed the Bishopps Secretary and other his Officers and servants in mourning cloakes to the number of betweene 20 and 30, in order 2 and 2.

4. After them followed the King at Armes and a Herald at Armes each of them being clad in mourning, and having

on, their coates of armes (*over their mourning*) embroidered with gold the one of them *holding* *bearing* in his hand the Bishopps Miter, and the other of them carryeing his Crosier.

5. After them followed the Herse (covered with the said black velvet cloath *or Pall* edged with white sarsenet hung round with his escocheons) borne by 6 poore men in gownes as aforesaid, on each side of the herse went 3 Doctors of Divinity who tooke hold of the herse cloath.

6. After them followed the Close mourners being the Bishopps Sonnes and other his neare relacions to the number of about 10; all covered over with mourning, noe hatts or capps on, onely *black* cloath care*le*sly lyeing *flatt* on their heades and but little of their faces seene, these alsoe went in order 2 and 2.

7. After them followed the Vice-Chancellor and Do^{rs} of Div: Law and Physick in their orders 2 and 2, in their scarlett robes and hoodes.

8. After them followed the Bachelors in Divinity in their gownes and hoodes haueing one or two Esqr Beadles in the head of them to a great number 2 and 2 in order.

9. And lastly followed all the Ma^r of Arts in their habitts and hoodes in order 2 and 2 *haueing as I take it the Vniversity Register carryeing a Beadles staffe in the head of them *.

Thus in their Orders they went to Pembroke Hall, where the Bishopp was laid in a vault in a stone Coffin under the upper *east* end of the new Chappell *there* which he caused to be built, and *which Chappell he himselfe* consecrated *himself the same* on St Matthews day Anno Domini 1665. D^{or} John Pearson then Ma^r of Trinity Coll: in Cambr'. made the Bishopps funeral Oration in the said new Chappell of Pembroke Hall the day of his funerall and buriall being Saturday the 11th May 1667.

All the said Do^{rs} &c. had each of them boxes of banquett to the number of 500 and to the value of about 5s. a box. *I think I was not present when the said funerall passed in the street, but I had the relacion of it.*

being Saturday dyed Mrs Tabor the wife of Mr Nicholas Tabor of St Clements parish in Cambr'. and shee was buryed on Munday following being the 15 July 1667.

[margin: July 13th Mrs Tabor wife of Nich: Tabor dyed]

Tewsday betweene 12 and one of the clock in the afternoone dyed Francis Wilford Do^r in Divinity, *Vicechancellor of the Vniversity of Cambridge* Deane of Ely, Archdeacon of Bedford, Ma^r of Bennett Colledge in Cambr': Rector of Halliwell and presented but not instituted or inducted to the Rectory of Landbeach, a man of a fatt corpulent body aged betweene 50 and 60 years.

[margin: July 16th Dr Wilford vice chancelor dyed.]

Tewsday *some out part of* The Towne of Ely was on fire *and great part of it was burnt downe* that is to say some little Tenements or Cottages in Newnham there to the number of 6 or 7 were burnt downe.

[margin: July 16th Fire in Ely]

Wednesday in the afternoone about 3 of the clock dyed Wm Wells Vintner one of the Aldermen of Cambr': and was buryed by Do^r Stephens in great St Maryes Church in the same graue where his first wife lay on Fryday the 26th July 1667.

[margin: July 24th Mr Wells dyed]

Thirsday hapned about 2 of the clock in the morning a fire in Southwarke at a Cookes house at the signe of the Shoulder of Mutton on St Margaretts hill, which consumed about 12 houses. I my selfe being then at London and see the smoake.

[margin: 25th July Fire in London]

being thirsday was Garlick fayre day, being the Assumpcion of our Lord.

[margin: 15 August]

being Fryday was the Grand Common day, at which was chosen the Maior and Bayliffes for the yeare following. At which time towards the choice came out of the Box Thomas Glorer and James Alders, who chose 12 electors and they 12 6 more to them and these 18, the Maior and Bayliffes. Att this eleccion wherein Phil. W^{ms} Sell Bird &c. were cheife were chosen Mr Richard Pettit the junior Alderman (saue Wm Pedder who came in Alderman that day) for New Elector Mayor for the yeare following, there being his Seniors Aldermen Robt Muriell John Cropley Nat. Crabb and Sam Moodey *who had the Goeby.* for Bayliffes were chosen, Sam.

[margin: August 16th Common Day for choice of maior & Bayliffes. Mayer & B. pro 1667 Rich. Pettit Mayor Sam. Richardson Jo. Tounesend Tho. Mace]

John More Richardson for the Bridgeward, Tounesend for the Talbooth,
Bayliffs
Mr Pedder Mr Mace for Reach fayre and John More Bayliffe O: For
made Coroners were chosen Mr Baron new Attorney and   of
Alderman. the 24^{ty}.

The same day was chosen Wm Pedder Alderman in the roome of Alderman Wells lately dead.

At the same day were chosen 2 24^{ty} men, one in the roome of Mr Cooper sen^r dead, and the other in the roome of Mr Pedder, the two 24^{ty} men then chose was first Thomas Dickenson, and last Mr Richard Pyke. The same day I had granted me, my lease of the little piece of wast on the backside of my 2 Tenem^{ts} next St Edwards Church.

The 26 Sept   On Thirsday being a called Common day, Mr Mace declaring he would not hold his said Bayliwick (he being priveledged *by* being in Priests Orders) he was for 40^s he freely paid to the Towne for a hansome come-off, was acquitted, and John More was chosen in his roome Bayliffe of Reach fayre.

26 of September being Thirsday dyed at Norwich Mr John Rhodes Preb: of Norwich and Rector of Bartonparva in Suffolk.

29th Sept   On Sunday, (being rayne all the day till about halfe an houre past 4 in the afternoone when it held up and the sun shined) being Michaelmas day, and Grand Common day, M^r
Mr Richard Pettit maior
Herring the then maior, and Mr Pettit then New Elect with most of the Aldermen and 24^{ty} in their scarlett and other proper habitts came in the morning to St Edwards Church where after divine service; preached Mr Sergeson our then minister; his text being the 6 Rom: 21 but it was not preached as the Maiors sermon, that being deferred till the Tewsday following, (the day *to* *on* which this grand common day was adjorned,) Mr Pettit was sworne this day after morning sermon at the Hall, to which place alsoe came the Vice Chancellor and swore him. &c.

October the first   On Tewsday, being the day to which the said Michaelmas
S:N: made Grand Common day was adjorned, I Samuel Newton was
of the 24^{ty} chosen to make upp the number of the Common Counsell

in the roome and place of M̃ Edward Potto brewer whose place was voyd by his living out of Cambr': by the space of one yeare.

Tewsday. This being grand Common day (by adjorne- Octob 1st ment) was the Michaelmas feast at the Hall.

First, in the morning *M̃ Pettit new mayor* the aldermen 24^ty and all others in their proper habitts being assembled and mett at the hall, from thence went to St Edwards Church where M̃ Pindar of Pembroke hall preached his text was   . After sermon all in their proper orders (the new Treasurers goeing first) went to the Hall, where (it being grand Common day) I, S. Newton, was chosen one of the Common Counsell in the roome of M̃ Edward Potto; some leases were then sealed, the Common day being ended soone after, dinner was served in, few strangers dined there none as I remember saue S̃ Tho: Sclater and his sonne Johnson. Dinner being ended all went home with M̃ Pettit then mayor, where we had 2 sugar cakes and a heart fashion sugar cake of M̃^rs Maris her making and euery one a glasse of sack, from thence wee all accompanyed home M̃ Herring the old mayor, where we had sack plenty and 2 sugar rolls. From thence the 24^ty *Towne Clerke* and Attorneyes (by my invitacion according to use ånd custome I being chosen that day of the Common Counsell) went to *M̃* Owen Mayfields at the Miter where I gaue them some bottles of sack, where we had alsoe the Vniuersity musick and soe fairely parted.

Thirsday (according to the time by his Matie formerly Octob. 10 prorogued) mett and assembled the Parliam^t.

[The following entry is in a child's hand, with lines ruled to guide it.]

I John Newton being in Coates this nineteenth day of October Anno Domini 1667 and not then full eight yeares old, wrote this by me

John Newton.

24th Nov. James Ayloffe baptized	Sunday Mr Martin Lister, Mrs Kath. Ayloffe and myselfe answered for James Ayloffe my cosin Ayloffs youngest sonne who was then baptized by Mr Wm Lynnet minister of Chesterton.
26 Nov. Mrs Wilford dyed	Tewsday Mrs Wilford the late Vice Chancelors widow departed this life.
26 Nov. my sister Ellis came to Cambr'	My sister Ellis came to Cambr' to visitt my wife being sick and shee with her husband went from hence on Fryday the 13th Dec. 1667.
15th December Ald. Simpson dyed & buryed.	Sunday about noone dyed Mr Rowland Simpson draper one of the Aldermen of Cambr', and was buryed in G^t St Maryes Church on Wednesday the 18th Dec. 1667 the mayor Aldermen and 24^ty at the funerall; borne to Church by 8 of the 24 whereof my selfe was one, Mr Jenner of Sidney preached his funerall sermon.
Decemb: 20th my wife had a sore fit of the Cholick.	Fryday had my wife a most greivous fitt of the stone cholick wch held her all that day and the next, insomuch that I much feared her death but God was pleased to deliuer her out of that extreame paine and torment *praysed bee his name therefore.*

[166$\frac{7}{8}$]

7th January Edward Wilson chaundler chose Ald^r man	Tewsday being the Grand Common day, and it being the next Tewsday after Twelfe day was Edward Wilson chandler chose Alderman in the roome of Alderman Simpson then lately dec^d, hee being present did not then accept of the same nor refuse it, but desired the 3 days limitted by the Order of the house to retourne his positive answer, the order enjoyning, that if in that time he did not accept of it, that he should presently pay 20^li. Soe the Common day was adiorned to the Thirsday afternoone sennitt being the 16th of this instant January 1667.
16 Jan. Mr Francis Jermin chose of the Common Counsell.	Thirsday being the day to wch the Common day was adjorned the same day Mr Edward Wilson chandler appeared at the Hall and tooke his place upon the bench as Alderman, and the same day was elected in the roome of his 24^ty mans place Mr Francis Jerman chandler, Mr Wilson caused the

Aldermen and 24^ty to come into the Parlor where they had each of them a cupp or two of sack and I think a sugar cake or 2: And Mr Francis Jerman he invited the 24^ty to the 3 Tunns and gaue them sack there, the same night, and at the same time Richard Pyke gaue a treatment of sack there as being 24^ty lately elected.

Wednesday about one of the clock in the afternoone dyed Mr William Pedder one of the Aldermen of the Towne of Cambridge; and was buryed in St Clements Church at the * very end of the * west end thereof against the middle Alley, on Fryday the 13th March 1667 the Maior Aldermen and 24^ty was at the funerall, and he was carryed by 8 of the 24^ty (myself being one that carryed); the bearers onely had gloues and each of them one of his escocheons, there being 8 upon his herse. Mr Wickham (his wifes sisters husband) preached his funerall sermon his text was the 6 Rom. 23. the wages of sin is death but the gift of God is eternall life.

11th March Mr Alderman Pedder dyed & buryed

1668.

Munday in the afternoone Mr Thomas Rippington of Wentworth in the Isle made and sealed his Will of wch he constituted John Bird his sole Executor and then as I take it after he had sealed his Will, in the presence of mee and John Craske, he delivered to Mr Bird aforesaid a certaine parchment writing with a seale, wch was folded up, and a seale sett upon it, and desired Margarett his wife to declare, that the writings as I take it the paper writings that were in the said parchment enclosed were sealed by her the said Margarett, and wch as he then said were not to be opened till * her death * after he was dead, he died at Mr Birds house in Cambr' the next day being the 31th March 1668 on Tewsday.

30th March Mr Reppington made his Will.

Munday being the Quarter Sessions, Mr Thomas Blackerby taylor went of of his high Constables place, Mr John Adams carpenter came on high Constable in his roome.

30th March Mr Blackerby went of High Constable.

7th Aprill This Common Day was adjorned to Thursday 9 Apr. and from thence continued and adjorned to Munday 13 Apr. Phil: Williams Ald^rman. Jos:Cooper *Bayliffe* Boyden & Sanderson *Treasurers*.	Hock Tewsday being generall Common day was chosen Philip Williams baker to be Alderman in the roome of Mr Wm Pedder dec^d. who then accepted thereof, and Mr Williams the same day gaue in the Parlor amongst the Alderm: and 24^ty seuerall bottles of sack onely, Treasurers then chosen were Boyden taylor who accepted, and Tho: Fox attorney who fined and passed offices for 10^li. Francis Challis Chandler chosen Treasurer who passed offices for 10^li fine, Cornelius Austin joyner chosen Treasurer, who passed all offices for 5^li. Dennis Cordiner chosen Treasurer who passed all offices for 10^li. John Witham who fined and passed offices, the same day was chosen Joseph Cooper butcher Bayliffe O. John Essex butcher chosen Treasurer who fined and passed offices, and last of all was chosen Sanderson Cordiner who accepted and held. Noe 24^ty man was chosen that day in the roome of Philip Williams, because he being the same day chosen to the Bench, it was the sense of some of the 24^ty, that one ought not according to the Orders to be chose till the Generall Common day next after that it happens any 24^ty mans place to be voyd.
17 Aprill Alderm: Ewin dyed.	Fryday morning dyed Mr John Ewin Chandler Alderman of Cambr': and was buryed on Sunday in the afternoone following being the 19th of Aprill 1668 in All Hallowes Church in Cambr': 6 of the Aldermen carryed him to Church who had gloues and Ribbons, All the 24^ty had gloues but not their wives, the Aldermens wives had gloves the service was 2 sugarcakes and 2 rolls, a cupp of clarrett, white and sack. Mr Puller of Jesus Coll: preached his funerall sermon his text was 1 Cor: 15 : 42. Soe alsoe is the Resurrection of the dead. It is sowen in Corrupcion, it is raysed in incorrupcion.
14 May Mr Roger *Thompson marryed*.	Thirsday in Whitson weeke was Mr Roger Thompson of Cambr' brewer singleman and Mrs Anne Margery of Chesterford widdow marryed at Stredwell in Essex. Mr Nath: Clarke gave her in marriage, they lay the first night at the said Mr Clarkes dwelling house at Chesterford, Mr Thompson

brought her home to Cambr' on Munday in the afternoone the 18 May 1668 in Mr Turners Coach at the Rose Tauerne in Cambr'.

Wednesday dyed Mrs Barbara Rhodes widdow at Do^r Herbert Astley his Lodgeing in Norwich, one of the Prebends there; shee made her Will and made Do^r Astley Executor, amongst other things in her Will shee gave mee and my wife each of us a ring of 20*s*: and gave 20^{li} to my sonne John Newton. *27th May M^{rs}Rhodes dyed.*

Tewsday the Mayor Aldermen and 24^{ty} went to Barnewell Abbey according to custome where they had 4 gamons of Bacon and stewed Pruens, the Towne sent wine, the Mayor onely went in his gowne with the Mace before him, the serjeants overnight went to the 24^{ty} to invite them from the Mayor. *June 16: Barnewell Abbey Collacion for the Towne.*

Fryday about noone dyed Mrs Morden the wife of Mr William Morden bookseller at Ware and was there buryed. *19th June Mrs Morden dyed*

Munday at a Common day Mr Willm Hinton Vintner came in Freeman by Mr Mayor as his freeman, and the same day passed all offices for the fine of 8^{li}. *22th June W^mHinton came in Freeman and passed offices.*

Wednesday dyed suddenly Tho: Graves Butler of Bennett Colledge in Cambr': I did see him at Mr Alderman Pettits dore within lesse then an houre before he was dead, and to mee seemed as well as he used to bee. *1st of July Tho: Graues dead*

Sunday preached at G^t St Maryes in Cambr'. both the Do^r Stillingfleetes, the sen^r in the morning and the Junr who was minister of St Andrewes Holbourne in London in the afternoone. both preached well but the Junior most eloquent the Senior his text in the morning was the 26 Acts 24: 25 and the Junior his text in the afternoone was in the 7 Luke 35. But Wisdome is justifyed of all her children; they both tooke their degrees of Do^{rs} of Divinity this publique Comencem^t 1668 Do^r Howarth Ma^r of Magd: being vicechanc'. M^r   of Christs and Mr Barnes of Peterhouse being Proctours. *5 July Do^r Stillingfleetes.*

August 9.
Ald. Chapman dyed.

August 17:
S. N. chose to the Bench in the roome of Alderman Edward Chapman deceased. Do* Howarth Master of Magdalen Coll was then Vice Chancellor and of Christs Coll. & M* Barnes of Peterhouse then Proctors John Buck Tho: Buck & Fr: Hughes then Beadles.

Sunday Alderman Chapman dyed at Barnett Waters and was buryed the day following at S* Andrewes Holbourne London.

Munday at a grand Common Day, (the proper day was the 16*th* Aug: being Sunday, but being Sunday (by order) when it falls on that day, it is to be on Munday following) when the Common day was opened and proclaymed M* Mayor before I came bid the Common Counsell make an eleccion to fill upp their number in the roome of Alderman Williams, and just upon their goeing into the Pantry (being the 24*ty* mans roome) I came into the Hall and went in with the 24*ty* to the eleccion and wee elected M* W*m* Hinton Vintner to be of the Common Counsell, when wee went in and had giuen our eleccion to the Mayor (M* Richard Pettit being then Mayor) M* Mayor declared that M* John Addams carpenter was by them chosen to the Bench in the roome of Alderman Ewin, and that they had chosen me S: N: to the Bench in the roome of Alderman Chapman dec*d*. M* Adams did tell them he thought himself unfitt, but was perswaded and did then take his place on the bench: For my selfe I tould them I was altogether unfitt for that place and desired them to thinke of some other person more fitt, M* Mayor tould mee I was chose with a full consent *and they thought mee fit, I tould them I *was the more sorry for it* did judge my selfe unfitt,* and *he* desired me to accept of it, I desired that I might haue time to consider of it 3 dayes according to the Order; which was giuen mee. The 24*ty* chose in the roome of M* Adams into the Common Counsell, M* Townesend *carpenter* baker, and I went into them and gaue my vote for him, but they tould me I being chosen to the bench might haue noe voate there, and they went into M* Mayor upon it, and he tould them I being chose to the bench I ought to haue no voyce, and soe *for that time* I left them and the Hall and came home. *and after some thoughts and prayers for Gods direction and that he would giue me a spiritt of humility, I opened the Bible to read, *wishing and praying that some passage of Scripture upon my opening* the booke might come to my veiw that might satisfy my doubts, and by prouidence I hapned and light on these words in the...Psalm and the.........I will prayse thee o lord for euermore because thou hast done it, and I will wayt on thy name, for it is good before thy saints, which place of Scripture...by prouidence coming to my ...ding made me conceiue it was by diuine appointment that I was chose to the Bench and this was............................... *

This same day was Alderman Nathaniel Crabb chose new elect. *after Common day was ouer, the mayor Aldermen and whole company went wth him to his house, where they were freely entertained with wine and Cakes.*

Tewsday about 9 of the clock in the Evening Mr Spalding and my selfe went to the 3 Tunns where Mr Richard Pettit mayor then was and in the Hall there in the presence of the said Alderman Spalding and Alderman Herring and did declare to Mr Mayor that I did accept of the choyse of Alderman that was made of mee at the last Common day. *August 18: I declared my acceptance of Alderman.*

Thursday I bought of Mrs Sarah Simpson widdow her husbands scarlett Gowne, and a plush seated new saddle with the bridle foot cloath and other riding furniture, for all wch I paid her the day following 9^{li} in full, for wch shee gaue me an acquittance wch is upon the file. *Aug: 20: I then bought of Mrs Simpson wid: her husbands furniture for Alderman.*

I made my 24^{ty} mans gowne serve for my Aldermans gowne and paid Mr Legg for 17 yards of lace for it at 1^s 6^d per yard 1^{li}:5^s:6^d for silke 3^s: 6^d for faceing the sleeves 1^s: and for altering and setting on the tufts 10^s I paid alsoe to Mrs Scott for 1^{li} and a halfe and 3 ounces of Naples Throse silke for the Tufts and making the Tufts accounting the silke at 1^{li}:7^s per li. (pound) 2^{li}:9^s: soe the whole charge of altering my gowne stood me in 4^{li} 9^s 0^d Mrs Scotts acquittance and Mr Leggs bill is on the file. *Aug: 25*

Munday being Bartholemew day, Mr Jermin lent me his horse, The Aldermen *in their scarlet Gownes* first on horseback goe to Mr New Elects, and there alight and haue a cupp *Aug: 24: Bartholomew day*

The Enterteinmt I gave as New Elect on Bartholomew day.

of sack and peece of great cake or a couple of sugar cakes, and likewise the 24^{ty} and all others goe thither first; and then all take Horse there and wth Mr New Elect ride to Mr Mayors who is ready at the dore to take horse and immediately ride to the fayre where reading the proclamacion usuall at the 2 usuall places vizt just beyond Stirbridge and on Honey Hill they ride in their orders home *to the Hall* and there alight, and goe in, and at the Aldermans Table Mr Mayor and Mr New Elect serues there onely, the service is sack by Each, and sugar cakes from each (2 *bottles of sack I think serves*) 2 rolls and 2 sugar cakes. After the service done there, Mr New Elect invites the Mayor Aldermen 24^{ty}, Bayliffs, Treasurers and Attorneyes to his house to dinner, and they all accompany him to his house, and there dyned all or the most in one roome, *and the mayor and Mrs New Elect sat at the upper and, Mr New Elect sat next his wife on the side.* at dynner wee had first 2 dishes of boyled chickens then a leg of mutton boyled, then a peece of rost beefe, then a mutton pasty, then a glasse of Clarrett round, then 2 couple of rabbetts, 2 couple of small wildfoule, and 2 dishes of tarts 3 in a dish. This was the enterteinement and by this time it was about 2 a clock soe the Aldermen putt of their scarlett gownes, and sent home for their black gownes, and went immediately to the Hall to the Common day, first the Aldermen went into the Parlor, and then considering what was fitt to be propounded, all the Aldermen went into the Hall, and then with them according to my juniority I tooke my place uppon the bench; when Common day was ouer, Mr Addams and my selfe being the last Common day chose to the bench, desired the Mayor Aldermen 24^{ty} and all other gownemen to goe into the parlor, and the freemen to tarry in the Hall to take a glasse of wine, wch they did, wee had betweene us 14 bottles of sack from the Miter, and then 3 quarters of a pound of tobacco with pipes candles and 3 flaggons of beere (for some desired to drinke beere). Note that the New Elect after his Eleccion alwayes in the afternoones accompanyes the Maior to Church, and alsoe goes along with the Maior to the Courts; and a serjeant allwayes attends him on the ryding dayes in the Fayre time to Mr Mayors.

The day before the fayre is proclaymed the Serjeant goes to every Alderman and his message is that Mr Mayor and Mr New Elect desires your company to the proclayming of the fayre to morrow about 8 of the Clock. On the proclayming day Mr Mayor sends a harnes man *about 7 in the morning* to euery Alderman to lett him know the certaine time he wilbe ready to goe to the fayre. *Stirbridge Fayre*

Munday being the Proclayming day for the fayre all the Aldermen in their scarlett gownes rides on horseback to Mr New Elects house and there alighting after salutacions to Mr New Elect haue a glasse of sack and cake and then Mr New Elect and the Alderman getting up on horseback ride to Mr Mayors, who is ready at his dore to gett up on horseback and presently doth, and then the Mayor New Elect and Aldermen with the Attorneys who ride before the Mayor and the 24^{ty} and Bayliffs and Treasurers behinde all in their gownes ride to the proclayming the fayre, and 1st they make a proclamacion in the hither end of the Duddery *and then ride through the duddery* 2^{ly} by the goldsmiths *and from hence turne into garlick row by that bookbinders*, 3^{rdly} in the midst of garlick row *and so goe all downe Garlick Row to the Water fayre*, 4^{ly} in the Water fayre and lastly on Honey hill and soe ride to the Mayors booth, where alighting and the Mayor and New Elect goeing upp to the Bench the Court is opened and proclaymed, and then immediately they goe upp to the Chamber and all but the Mayor and New Elect putt of their gownes till dinner time and then putt them on againe and after dinner off againe Mr Mayor setts next the window and Mr New Elect next the Wall, the Mayor giues thanks if noe minister present; when the business of the Court is over, they putt on their gownes againe and soe home every one leaving Mr Mayor as his way leades him to his seuerall home. *7 Sept' Proclayming day for the fayre.*

Teusday being the next day after the fayre is proclaymed *8 Sept*

Serjeant or Harnesman	and soe afterwards the New Elect allwayes comes to the mayors house *attended by a Serjeant or harnesman* then the Mayor New Elect and Aldermen present rides away to the fayre.
8 Sept Porter at Trin: Coll: from the Mayor at his vissiting the Judges 1ˢ.	Tewsday being the day Sʳ Matthew Hales Kᵗ Lord Cheife Baron of his Maᵗⁱᵉˢ Exchequor and Judge of Assize came to hold the Assizes. whome at Trin: Coll: the Mayor Recorder and Aldermen did visit, when the Mayor went away out at the foregate he gave as is usuall to (the Serjeant to giue) the Porter of the Coll. 1ˢ.
19 Sept	Saturday notice by the Serjeant was given to all the Aldermen that the Sessions was on Tewsday following being the 22ᵗʰ day of this instant Sept.
22ᵗʰ Sept Sessions	Tewsday was the quarter Sessions at the Hall, where all the Aldermen ought but many did not appeare, Mʳ *Spalding* Crabb being Mʳ New Elect, Mʳ Spalding Mʳ Finch, Mʳ Cropley, Mʳ Moodey, Mʳ Moody, and Mʳ Wilson did appeare, and I was there about an houre, till sent for away upon earnest busines. *Mʳ Mayor onely is in his scarlet robes, the Aldermen in their black gownes. Mʳ James Robson and Mʳ John Bird chose then Cheife Constables.*
26ᵗʰ Sept an obijt sermon	Saturday Thomas Harper the serjeant came to me to giue me notice that to morrow being the Sunday before Michaelmas was an obijt sermon, and that on Tewsday next being Michaelmas day Mʳ Mayor desired my company.
29 Sept':	Tewsday Michaelmas day in the morning presently after 8, all the Aldermen in their Scarlett Robes first goe to Mʳ New Elects, (Mʳ Crabb then being New Elect) whither alsoe all the 24ᵗʸ and gownemen comes, there euery of us had a glasse of sack and great peaces of cake, from thence after halfe an houres stay wee went with Mʳ New Elect all in order to Mʳ Mayors, and there haueing a cupp of beere wee went all to Church (Trinity Church,) and after sermon to the Hall *the M. and Ald.* goeing first into the Parlor and propounding and considering what was fitt to be propounded at the Common day, and within a qʳ of an houre went into the Hall and the Common day being opened, there was pro-

pounded what in the parlor was considered fitt to be propended, which done, presently they went to sweare officers; and first Mr *Crabb* Pettit then Mayor he declared that he had finished his yeare and that was all he said *then the serjeants laid downe all their Maces on the Table.* Then Mr Crabb New elect, made a short speech; and said Gentlemen I am (though unworthy) chose to this Office, that wch I shall desire of you is cheifly and in the first place to ayme and to promote the glory of God, then our duty to the King and the tranquility of each other wch obserued I shalbe the more encouraged and better assisted to discharge my duty wch I shall...*withall* dilligence endeavour, and then the Recorder first gaue the said Mr New Elect his Oath as Mayor, and then by virtue of a Comission out of Chancery for that purpose gaue him the Oath of Alleigance and Supremacy, and another Oath for his being Justice of the Peace for that yeare of his Mayoraltye. Then were the Bayliffs for that yeare sworne, then the new Treasurers. Then the Corroners, Mr John Cropley then Alderman being sworne one of them, which he very much disliked, and would have bin excused from it, but it would not be granted. Mr Robt Drake the Attorney was the other Corroner then sworne *and then were the Serjeants sworne and afterwards take up their Maces.* Then did Mr Mayor send 2* of the senior Common Counsell to St Maryes where the ViceChancellor was to lette him understand, he was ready to receive the Oath from him to be given and accordingly the Vice-Chancellor came with the Proctors and 3 or 4 of the Doctors and in the Hall by the Proctors gaue the mayor the oath usuall not to infringe the Libertyes of the Vniuersity wch done Mr Mayor invited them into the parlor to a glasse of wine, wch being served them they departed. Then did Mr Mayor with the Aldermen goe into the Hall and adjorne the Common day till Wednesday cum sennitt and the Common day for that day ceased. Then Dinner being ready, they went to it and what doctors were there satt at the upper end next the old and new Mayor, all others of lower degree satt below the Aldermen.

Mr New Elects speech just before his oath-taking.

* it seemes it is most usuall to send 2 of the Bayliffs

Dinner being ended after Tobacco being taken which was not aboue halfe an houre after dinner new Mr Mayor invited all *w* home with him, and there haueing a glasse of wine and 2 sugar cakes and a Roll, old Mr Mayor invited all whome to his house where wee had sack and sugar cakes and soe departed to our owne homes. Note that *after* Mr Mayor is sworne, yet the old Mayor goes euen with him and from his house to his owne home first Mr Recorder being next him.

7th Oct. Wednesday at one in the afternoone (to which Michaelmas Common day was adjorned) was by Mr Moody produced a Letter from the Councell board directed to the Sheriffe of Cambridge sheire, requiring the more strict putting in execucion the Act concerning Corporacions made in the 13th of K^s Charles the 2^d and particulerly for all officers and for the taking of the 3 Oathes therein expressed, and accordingly I declared upon the bench* that I was willing and ready to take the same, but they would not administer the same making some doubt whither the Aldermen were to take them, the same day was propounded how the K^s and Queene should be enterteyned if they came, it was determined each of them should be presented with a peece of plate, both to be to the value of about 50^{ll}, to that end and for the allowing Mr Mayor to keepe a free table for that time at the hall 60^{ll} was taken out of the chest of Mrs Knights for money to be againe thither retourned as soone as it might be raysed and 40^{ll} more was granted to be p^d the mayor by the Treasurers for that service. The same day was sealed the Lease to Pembroke Hall of the passage into St Tho: Leyes, the Common day was adjorned to Munday following to one in the afternoone.

* All the Ald^{r}men was then present except Mr Spalding Mr Finch & Mr Muriell

9th Oct. Fryday Alderman Moodey was sent up by the Corporacion to London to provide presents for the King and Queene who were expected to be heere on Saturday the 17th Oct. 1668 and he sent downe word, that most in fashion was a peece of plate called a Salver *holding about 2 qts.* for the K^s and a silver baskett for the Queene; the salver comeing to about

Mr Moody appointed to London to buy a present for the King & Queene

30ᵘ and the baskett about 20ᵘ: but the King and Queene changeing their resolucion concerning comeing there was an end of that and of the Vniuersity banquet, which was said they had provided at London to the value of about 100ᵘ and the Vniuersity intending to present the Kᵍ with his fathers workes, and the Queene with a payre of gloues.

Munday at one in the afternoone at a Common day to this time adjorned came in *Benj.* Spence the Chaundler free, and had his freedome gratis as being apprentice to James Alders. his Indentures were made for 7 yeares, but James Alders *there* confest he served him but onely the 5 last. Alderman Richard Pettit was then in the Parlor by virtue of a Commission directed to Mʳ Spalding and Mʳ Herring sworne a Justice of Peace for the Towne and Vniuersity of Cambr', Alderman Finch was alsoe by the same Comission to be sworne in like manner a Justice of the Peace but he went away and would not be sworne.   *12ᵗʰ Oct. An adjorned Common day.*

Thirsday my sister Ellis and my sonne John Newton went from hence to Waddesden and my cosin Susan Ellis stayed heere, who came hither on Tewsday 13 Oct. 1668.   *15ᵗʰ October Jo. Newton*

Saturday before Fryday night dyed Doʳ   Howarth Maʳ of Magdalen Colledge and then Vice-Chauncellor of the Vniversity of Cambridge.   *16ᵗʰ October Dᵒʳ Howarth Vice-Chancellor dyed.*

Munday Dʳ Fleetwood Provost of Kings chose Vice-Chancellor for the Remainder of Dʳ Howarths yeare.   *19ᵗʰ Oct. Dʳ Fleetwood Procan. for remainder of that year.*

Fryday according to notice overnight this morning about 8 of the clock I went in my black gowne to Mʳ Mayors house where alsoe mett Alderm: Finch, Alderm: Herring and Alderm: Muriell, with 3 or 4 of the 24ᵗʸ and Bayliffs and Towne Clerke, all in their Gownes, their wee were very well treated with a plate of sliced cakes and strong beere and sugar and nutmegg, and when the schoolebell rang, all of us went to Gᵗ Sᵗ Maryes into the vestrey staying there till the   *23 Oct. Paving Leet.*

Vice-Chancellor came who came not into the Vestrey but *being in black habitt* went immediately into his *usuall* seat in the Chancell, and then the Mayor Aldermen &c. followed taking their places on the other side in the noblemens seat. After all sett Mr Whyn the Vniuersity Register by Titus Tillett the under Beadle calls 12 persons sumoned to be there to be sworne for the paving Leet, and then the Towne Clerke 12 for the Towne, which being impannelled are all sworne by the Vniuersity Register, then the Vice-Chancellor giues them a charge that according to their oath they make a due presentment.

Then the Vice-Chancellor and the rest of that body arise from their seats and goe into the Vestry and putt on their Scarlett Roabes and from thence retourne into the Chancell with the Beadles before them and take their places at the upper end of the Chancell *next* *neare* the Table on Formes for that purpose appointed being made a Quadrangle and the Doctors with him, the proctors sitting behinde the Vice-Chancellor upon a forme next the Table, and then comes the mayor Aldermen &c. and he takes his place at the upper end of one of the *north* side formes next unto the Vice-Chancellor (the Vice-Chancellor sitting at the end forme) *and the Aldermen sitt next the mayor, or next the Doctors on the other side* and then first the Proctors sware 2 of the Senior Aldermen present, to hold true fidelity to the King &c. and then is called the Black Assembly and sworne 2 for every parish that are Townesmen, (priviledged persons clayming to be exempted) which being done for the whole Towne, then are sworne the serchers for leather, and these Oathes for the black Assembly and leather serchers are giuen by the Proctors, but called ouer by the Towne Clerke, when they are sworne, the Vice-Chancellor giues them that are sworne to understand the nature of an Oath and what it is : it is to call God Angells and men to witnes to the truth, and if we doe not performe, then we call Heaven and earth to beare witnes of our perjury and falshood and soe *giving the paving leet a weeks time to retourne their presentments* dismissed them and then the Vice-Chancellor and the rest of their body departed, and soe the mayor and the rest of the Towne went home with Mr Mayor as many as pleased whom he invited all in to drinke, but none but the Aldermen went in, and taking a pipe of Tobacco and cup of beare departed.

Munday night was Port at Mr Pettits the last mayor, where the Bayliffes Treasurers and their wifes supt.   *2 Nov. Port*

Tewsday morning Mr mayor sent a serjeant to mee as he did to the rest of the Aldermen, desiring our Companyes at the Hall at 8 a clock in the morning on the 5th day of November being Thirsday next in our Scarlett Gownes to goe with him to Church to Great St Maryes to the Sermon.   *3 Nov.*

Thirsday according to former notice wee in our Scarlett, and the 24^{ty} in their Gownes went to the Hall and from thence presently went with Mr Mayor to G^t St Maryes to Common prayer and tarryed till sermon ended, and from thence all went to the Hall where wee all and the 24^{ty} dyned, to dinner wee had 2 leggs of veale and bacon, a large peece of roast beefe a foreline and a hinder line of porke and 3 couple of rabbetts and about 2 bottles of Clarrett, after dinner Mr Mayor with some of the Aldermen went to Barnewell to veiw a way there out of repayre and soe home.   *5 Nov. Scarlett day*

Sunday there were 2 obijt sermons one at Trinity namely Mr Fanns, and the other at G^t St Maryes namely Mr Foxtons and wee went to the Hall and had Cakes and wine.   *8 Nov. Obijts two. Fan & Foxton*

Wednesday Richard Herring the sonne of Alderman Herring draper, did drowne himselfe as it is thought betweene 6 and 7 in the morning before it was light betweene Garrett hostle bridge and Trinity Coll. Tenniscourt, he had bin at play at dice the night before being Tewsday night at John Dods at the Red Heart in the Petticury and lost (as was thought) there with a London gamester and cheater above 100^{li} which as was thought was the onely reason he offered vyolence to himselfe, the money was said to be taxmoney received by him for Captain Story, *he was buryed in the South Churchyard of G^t St Maryes the same night.*   *11th Nov. Richard Herring drowned himselfe*

25 Dec.
Scarlett
day

Fryday X'tmas day the *maior and* Aldermen goe to Church in Scarlett. There being a Comunion that day at our Church S' Edwards, I went thither in the morning in my black gowne (neither M' Spalding nor M' Pettit were at Church) and I received the holy Sacrament of the Lords * body * *supper*, the same day received alsoe Do' Stoyt old M' Buck &c. in the afternoone when the bell rang at Great S' Maryes I went in my scarlett gowne thither to Church as did the rest of the Aldermen in scarlett. *Do'* Baldero the Vice-Chancellor preacht and made a good sermon on these words in the 19 Luke and 10 The sonne of man is come * into the world * to seeke and to save that which was lost.

31 Dec.
X'tmas present to
M' Mayor

Thirsday being New Yeare Eve, I sent into M' Mayors about 4 of the Clocke in the afternoone my present, which was a westfalia ham which weighing 10^{li} at 1^s per li cost 10^s alsoe 2 capons cost 4^s and 1 Turkey which cost 2^s : 8^d in all 16^s : 8^d. The *M'* Mayor then had not sent to invite any of the Aldermen nor were any that day invited.

166$\frac{8}{9}$.

2 Jan.
Inviting to
M' Mayors
feast

Saturday in the Duske of the evening came Tim. Marsh in the name of M' Mayor and M'^{rs} Maris to invite me and my wife to dine *there* with them the Munday following being the 4th Jan. 1668.

4 Jan.
M' Mayors
Feast

Munday according to former invitacion I and my wife went with M' Spalding in our Gownes to dine with the Mayor, at which dinner dined Strangers onely Sir Tho. Sclater and Do' Stoyt, all the 12 Aldermen were present, but not above halfe of their wives, seuerall tarryed supper. at my comeing away I gaue Mary their mayd 2^s.

12th Jan.
Grand
Common
day

Tewsday next after Twelfe being Grand Common day M' Ewins sonne chandler past offices for the fine of 8^{li}: a Lease for 80 y^{rs} or thereabouts was granted to St Johns Coll. of a peece of enclosed ground lyeing at the end of Harrow Lane in Barnewell late Smiths and after Goodwins *being next the footbridge and feilde* for 1ˢ per annum rent, and for the fine of 3ˡⁱ. Alsoe a lease was granted of Harpers boothes in Stirbridge fayre *lying at the upper end of the hop fayre* to Sam. Richardson for 21 yeares for 50ˢ per annum rent, when there is a fayre, and 25ˢ rent when there is noe fayre, he paid noe fine. The forfeiture is onely for want of payment of this rent of 50ˢ: but noe forfeiture for the 25ˢ onely a Covᵗ from him for payment of both according as the fayres or noe fayres fall out. Alsoe a lease granted to Peter Dent Appothecary of a peece of wast ground on the backside of his dwelling house at the end of his garden extending from the Kings Ditch in breadth into his garden 17 feet or thereabouts and in length along the Kings Ditch being the whole breadth of his garden 40 and odd feet. To hold for 60 yeares for 1ˢ per annum. The rent formerly being but 4ᵈ per annum and he paid the fine of 20ˢ. then alsoe was propounded a lease of a slaughterhouse for Ric. Norman the butcher to be renewed and a Committee appointed to veiw it and make report. Alsoe was granted to Mʳ Maior license to plant trees on the wast at the Castle end on the banke next Mʳ Storyes ground. Alsoe notice given by the Maior to the Treasurers that they pay noe money without the Counsellors hands and taking receipts to be orderly produced upon the passing their accounts. Alsoe that all freemen take speciall notice of that part of their oathes that enjoynes secrecy for the Towne affayres Mʳ Maior intimating that they were too much discouered. Mʳ Maior required of the Towne Clerke a Catalogue of all the books evidences and writings of the Towne in his hands as it is enjoyned for him to make *as appeares* in a great booke page the 45 or 145 and alsoe desired Mʳ Lawes more constant company and attendance. Also Mʳ Mayor appointed Auditors for Treasurers accompts whose names all I doe not well remember, A Lease of the Mills alsoe was granted to Alderman Williams and Mʳ Townesend to hold for yeares, and out of the first 2 yeares rent they to be allowed 20 or 22ˡⁱ paid by them for repayres.

13 Jan. Notice of the sessions	Wednesday, Thomas Harper serjeant came to me to giue me notice the quarter Sessions was on Munday next at 8 in the morning.
18 Jan. Sessions	Munday was the Towne Sessions, but I was not there, for I conceived it not convenient because I was uncertaine whither I was in Commission for the Gaole deliuery.
19 Jan. Mr Mayor feasts his neighboures.	Tewsday Mr Crabb mayor made a feast inviting his neighbours about him.
22 Jan. Cosin Frohocks Children dyed	Fryday morning dyed John Frohock eldest sonne of my cosin John Frohock.
24 January	Sunday morning dyed *Margaret* Frohock daughter of my cosin John Frohock.
25 Jan.	both buryed on Munday night in St Maryes Church in one grave.
24 Jan. Alderman Ranewes obijt Sermon	Sunday in the afternoone after St Maryes was Alderman Ranewes obijt sermon preached, but neither the Mayor nor Aldermen were at it *nor doe take any notice of it*.
29 Jan. Kings Fast Day given notice of by order of Mr Mayor	Fryday came Tho: Harper the Serjeant to me from Mr Mayor in his name desiring me to be at Mr Mayors house on the morrow morning by 8 of the Clock to accompany him to Gt St Maryes, it being the day of fast for the Kings suffering: and alsoe he gave me notice of an obijt sermon on Sunday next to bee at Trinity.
30 Jan. Kings Fast Day	Saturday I went to Mr Mayors about halfe an houre after 8, but hee and such of the Aldermen as had bin at his house that morning, were just gone to St Maryes, and I went after, where wee had the service for that day appointed all said but the Letany and the Offertory prayers and then the Bell rang after which done the Vice Chancelor &c came, and then the Letany was sung in the Chancell and Do^r Duport Master of Magdalen preached then on this text the 7th Acts and the last verse, these words Lord lay not this sin to their charge

* Mr Nath Crab maior

and made a very exelent sermon; after sermon ended, the Aldermen went from their seat with the mayor to the Churchyard and their euery one parted to his own home.

Sunday, being the Sunday before Candlemas was preached (at G^t St Maryes after Trinity Lecture done in the afternoone) the Obijt sermon of Richard Chevin late Burgesse of Cambridge who gaue Clement Hostle to the Towne, To the intent that 2 sermons should be preached yearly in y^t parish Church where the Mayor for the time being lived, the one upon the Sunday next before Candlemas and the other upon the Sunday next before Hallomas and that 6^{li} ˢ. ᵈ. should be namely ˡⁱ ˢ. ᵈ. thereof to the minister that preacht and the rest to the poore, Mr Sergeant of Kings preacht this sermon, This day the Aldermen had notice to be at Trinity Lecture and from thence to goe to St Maryes which accordingly as many as came did, with the Mayor who was at Trinity Lecture, Mr Edwards the Lecturer was not invited to the Hall, neither St Maryes reader of the prayers, but after the Obijt Sermon was done Mr Mayor sent a serjeant to meet Mr Serjeant as he came downe out of the pulpitt to invite him to the Hall.

31 Jan. Mr Chevins Obijt

Mr Mayor at the Hall had of this Obijt money 3^s which he gaue to the poore prisoners, and the 3 senior Aldermen 1^s per peice which they kept.

Wednesday Mr Hughes Esquire Beadle and my selfe were godfathers to Roger Thompson sonne of Mr Roger Thompson and of Anne his wife and Mrs Merchant and my cosin Clerke were godmothers, the said Roger the sonne was this day baptized at home in her chamber by Mr Christopher Bainbrigg of Christs Colledge.

Feb. 3. Roger Thompson Junr baptized

Thirsday night dyed Susanna Mayfield daughter of Owen Mayfeild and buryed on Sunday following the 7th Feb. 1668.

Febr. 4 Susan Mayfield dyed

Saturday about 4 or 5 in the afternoone dyed Mrs Goad widdow the Relict of Do^r Goad late Kings Professor at Law in the Vniversity of Cambridge deceased.

Febr. 6 Mrs Goad dyed

* Mr Nath. Crabb Mayor

Feb. 9 Dan. Harthorne dyed	Tewsday morning dyed Daniell Harthorne porter and gardiner of Pembroke Hall.
March 12 Sam¹ Frohock butcher dyed	Fryday dyed Sam¹. Frohock butcher at his house in the Fenns neare Awdrey bridge in Haddenham parish and was buried in Trinity Church in Cambridge on Sunday the 14 Mar. 1668 on the backside at the further end of the Aldermans seat.
March 11 Mr Clench dyed	Thursday dyed Mr John Clench of Bottisham.
March 18 Judges visited	Thursday morning a serjeant came to me, desiring me from Mr Mayor to accompany him and the Aldermen to the Judges at their comeing in, in the afternoone, just upon the Judges comeing in, notice is given by the Serjeants to the Aldermen, and then goeing to Mr Mayors house *in our gownes* haueing there a cupp of Ale wee from thence went to Trinity Colledge to salute and visitt the Judges being Judge Hale and Judge Windham where haueing complemented them, wee presently take our leaues and, according as our way leades to our home wee take our leave of Mr Mayor. At Mr Mayors passing through Trinity Colledge gate, he gives the porter 1^s or what he pleases more.
March 21th William Mathew marryed to my servant Anne	Sunday William Mathew shoomaker marryed at Allhallowes in Cambridge by Mr Puller minister there, unto Anne Beecham my mayd servant.

1669.

Mar. 25 Newes brought that my sone Sam¹ was dead	Thirsday in the afternoone about 3 of the clock my wife being but a little while come from Nurse Muns, where shee had bin most part *of the day* with my sone Samuel being very weake, word was sent and brought to me and my wife by Nicholas (Nurses man) that Samuel was dead, he goeing away in a very tedious fitt *he* then had, but within a quarter of an houre after, Frances brought us word that he was come to life againe.

Katherine my mayd servant came this Thirsday into my service for 48ˢ per annum wages. *March 25. My mayd Kath. came*

On Fryday in the afternoone about 7 of the clock departed this life Samuel Newton my third sonne, he fell sick on Munday last in the afternoone, and was buryed in Sᵗ Edwards South Chancell in Cambr. at the upper end under a marble stone on the day following being Saturday at night the 27 March 1669. *March 26. My sone Samˡ. departed this life*

Easter day in the morning being a Comunion at our Church I went thither in my black Aldermans gowne and soe did Mʳ Pettit, but in the afternoone as the rest of the Aldermen did, I went in my Scarlet Gowne to Gᵗ Sᵗ Maryes, as it is usuall to doe. *April 11. Scarlet day*

Tewsday being Hock Tewsday and Grand Common Day were chosen William Hurrell Cordiner who refused and fined for Treasurer, alsoe was then chosen for Treasurers Thomas Nicholson smith and Matthew Blackley baker, it was then ordered that for the future the order for registring apprentices be revived, a Lease to be made for 21 yeares was granted to Richard Norman senior of his slaughterhouse for the fine of 3ˡⁱ there being 11 yeares anew putt in *This Common Day was adjorned to Wednesday 12 May next.* *Aprill 27. Treasurers chose*

Saturday morning betweene 10 and 11 of the Clock came *from Newmarket up the Peticury* to the Rose Taverne in Cambridge the Prince of Tuscany in his Coach and 6 horses with a postilion, there came also along with him 2 other Coaches, he then was about the age of 28 yeares a proper man very thick *in person* and very swarthy in his favour he came apparelled in the then english mode an ordinary stuffe vest and tunick *of a sadish Couller* siluer buttons, Mʳ Mayor and the Aldermen in their scarlett and the bayliffs Treasurers and 24ᵗʸ in their Gownes, went imediately after he was out of his Coach to visitt him which was in the Chamber at the Rose next Sᵗ Michaells Churchyard (Mʳ Recorder was absent) and Mʳ Crab being then out of Towne and at London, Mʳ Herring as Deputy Mayor with the Aldermen presented *May 1ˢᵗ Prince of Tuscany visited by the Towne*

* Mʳ Nath. Crabb Mayor

themselves to him and Mr Mayor after due obeysance to his person spoke and tould him, that he was very welcome to the Corporacion and assured him that to the utmost of *their* *our* power he should be as safe whilest he was heere as in his owne dominions; the Prince (untill *Sir Barnard Gascoigne* his interpreter gaue him to understand what Mr *Deputy Mayor* had said) stood with his hat on his head but then when he understood what had bein spoke he *pulled of his hat and stood beare and* by his interpreter thankt Mr Mayor for that Civility and said it was a fine Towne he liked it well, Mr Mayor further desired that his highnes would hono^r the Corporacion at the Guildhall that they might there treat him, he by his interpreter thankt them but said *he would* *it was his resolucion* not be chargeable to any place where he came and soe Mr Mayor giving a low Congey and the Aldermen took their leaves and came away.

The Vniversity

The Uniuersity alsoe soone after the mayer and Alderman had left him did visit him vizt Do^r Gunning master of St Johns and Kings Professor of Divinity *in scarlet* with all the noblemen in the Vniuersity in their Gownes conducted the Prince from the Rose to the Schooles, they goeing before him and undergraduates being all the way in good order placed on both sides from the Rose to the Schooles and Bachelors in their hoodes from Mr Mordens house to the hither end of the Regent walke, and from thence Master of Arts to the Schooles all in their habits, the Vice Chancellor and Do^rs in their scarlet met the Prince in the middle of the Regent walke and soe conducted him to the Regent house, but the Prince tooke noe degree, 2 or three of his nobles tooke the degree of Do^r of Lawes or some such like and then went out of Fellow Commoners about 20 Master of Arts; thence the Prince went to his Inne and dyned, and then againe to the schooles where there was a Phylosophy Act and from thence went to Kings Coll. Chappell where they had a musick devertisement, from thence he went by the Regent walke all along the street on foot to St Johns Coll.

* Mr Crabb Mayor Do^r Boldero Vicechancellor

and there was a little while and from thence came to Trinity Coll., where *at the first rayles* schollers, Bachelors and Master of Arts of that Coll. were orderly placed all along the first walke on both sides *to the Lodge* and at the first rayles Mr Lynnet met the Prince and conducted him to the Crosse passage before the Masters Lodgeing *against the King and Queens Hostle* and there mett him Mr Dove fellow of the College and made a short speech to the Prince and afterwards there the Master and Seniors in their habitts received him and shewed him the Colledge Hall and the further Court and soe brought him to the Masters Lodge, * where after a banquet had * *and then* they went to the Comedy house where they had a Comedy called * Nola * calculated or composed for the Italian meridian which lasted till about 9 at night * He went * he *went* seemed to like the Comedy very well and as the usuall manner is did clap his hands at it, he went from hence on Sunday morning the 2 May 1669. At his departure he gaue 10^s to Tom Holyday the Towne Cryer who at his comeing in directed the Coaches which way to come to the Market place; els he gaue not either officers or servants of either body anything that I heard of worth taking notice of.

About the 4th or 5th of May 1669 dyed Mr John Byng of Grancester.

Wednesday, to which day the last Comon day was adjorned and continued, Mr Mayor declared that Matthew Blackley had given his answer that he would not hold Treasurer, soe the Electors made a new eleccion of Dickenson to be Treasurer who desired time 2 or 3 dayes to consider, and soe the Common day was continued till Tewsday next. This day came in freemen David Hall butcher as being a freemans sonne, and James Sanders butcher as being a freemans apprentice.

May 12

In the parlor Mr Mayor bound seuerall persons ouer for putting in their cattle upon the Common before mayday. The forme of the Recognizance was thus to them seuerally repeated:

—— You doe acknowledge to owe unto our Soueraigne Lord the King 20ˢ to be leavyed upon your lands and tenements goodes and chattells. The condicion is that you shall appeare at the next generall Sessions of the Peace to be holden for this Towne.

He bound ouer alsoe Robert Bell one of the Pounders to prosecute and his Recognizance was alsoe 20ˢ and the condicion that he should appeare the next Sessions to giue in evidence against such as he did know to putt on any cattell on the Commons before mayday.

May 15
Invitacion to Reach fayre

Saturday morning came Tho: Harper Serjeant in the name of the mayor and Bayliffe of Reach to desire my Company with Mʳ Mayor to Reach fayre betweene 6 and 7 on next Munday morning.

May 17.
Reach fayre

Munday morning about 7 of the clock, all the Aldermen repayre to Mʳ Mayors, where there is Ale and Cake, and sack, euery one haueing dranke, take horse at the dore, Mʳ Mayor rides in a black Clock, his horse a breast plate and bridle and crooper answerable with brasse stirrups, at Reach he giues to the horse looker 6ᵈ to the watchmen 1ˢ and soe being accompanyed to his house home where the company nowe alighting all take there leaues.

May the 18.
Common day

Teusday was Common day to which time the last Common day was adjorned, but I was not there. *Then was brought and paid in the 100ˡⁱ that Alderman Chapman gaue in his Will to the Towne to be yearly for an obijt sermon about Easter and other pious and charitable purposes.*

May 21.
Samˡ. Ellis admitted in Tr. Coll

Fryday in the afternoone about 3 of the Clock was my cosin Samˡ Ellis admitted into Trinity Colledge in Cambridge which was the first time he put on a blue gowne and I my selfe helpt him on with it.

May the 27.
Mʳ. Botwright dyed

Thirsday dyed Mʳ John Botwright Attorney of the Towne Court and was buryed the day following being Fryday the 28 May 1669.

May 29.

Saturday being the day of the Kings birth and retourne was solemnely obserued in Towne, there being noe market,

* Mʳ Crabb mayor

proclamacion for that purpose being the Saturday before made to prohibit it according to former notice on Thirsday, the Aldermen in their Scarlett, and the 24^ty Bayliffs and Treasurers in their Gownes, about 8 in the morning repayred to the Hall from whence the Mayor and whole company went to prayers to G^t St Maryes, after which was done and the Letany sung and some further prayers said that are appointed, preached Do^r Boldero Vice-Chanceller his Text was in Psalme , Thou hast delivered thy servant David from the edge of the sword. He made a very exelent Sermon shewing the greatnes of Gods mercy in the Kings deliuerance and restoracion and exhorting us to our duty of thankfullnes by our good conversacion and loyalty to our soueraigne. From sermon Mr Mayor and all the rest of our body went to the Hall where at the Towne charge there was a very good dinner provided to which were invited by Mr Mayor Mr Edwards minister, Mr Gipps minister of St Maryes, Mr Vincent and Mr Story, wee all dyned at one table in the Hall. There was a great dish of saltfish, a fayre legg of mutton, a legg of veale and bacon, a very large peece of rost beefe, a fore quarter of lambe and salletts, 2 capons and a dish of young rabbetts and about 6 or 8 bottles of claret, and dinner being done wee tooke Tobacco a little while, and then departed. After wee came downe from the Hall Mr Mayor beckoned the Aldermen to goe home with him, and soe wee did, and there satt awhile and drank *......* and soe euery one went to their owne home.

Kings birth and retourne
Scarlett day
Do^r Boldero preached

In the afternoone came Jo. Bridge the sergeant to me from Mr Mayor desiring my company at Mr Mayors house on Wednesday next betweene 12 and one of the clock in my Cloake to accompany him to Mr Butlers at Barnewell as yearely the custome is.

Munday the 14 June Notice from Mr Mayor to goe to Barnwel Abbey

Wednesday betweene 1 and 2 met the Aldermen that is to say Mr Finch, Mr Cropley, Mr Moodey, Mr Williams Mr Adams and my selfe (and Mr Tifford met at Barnewell) at

June 16

* Mr Crabb Mayor

Barnewell Abbey Collacion

Mr Mayors house with the Treasurers old and new elect, the Bayliffs and seuerall of the 24{ty}, from whence the Mayor in his Gowne with Marsh the Serjeant in his Gowne and with the mace, before the Mayer, the Aldermen and rest in their Cloakes went to Barnewell Abbey to Mr Butlers * where * *who complemented us and afterwards* Mrs Butler came whom the mayor and Aldermen onely saluted, there at Mr Butlers charge all the company had Gamon of Bacon, creame and stewed pruens and strong beere and cake the Towne sent wine and sugar and soe after the Treat done the company went away from thence, nothing being given to the servants by Mr Mayor or any els, then we went to the mayors booth in Midsomer fayre and dranke some cans of beere, where the mayor was 1^s the Aldermen 6^d per peice and from thence went home accompanying the Mayor till the way to our seuerall houses tooke us away where we left him, nothing but a tankard of small beere at Mr Mayors before we went from thence.

22 June Midsommer fayre

Tewsday being St Audreyes Eve 2 days before Midsomer day, in the morning all the Aldermen in their Cloakes mett about 9 in the morning at Mr Mayors house, where wee and the rest of the Company had sack small beere and Cake, a great Carroway Cake being sett upon the Table, euery one tooke what they pleased. Mr Mayor and the Sergeant and Bayliffs in their Gownes and the Aldermen and 24{ty} in their Cloakes went from Mr Mayors to the fayre to the Booth there, when they came there Mr Mayor putt off his black Gowne, and hee and all the Aldermen putt on their scarlett Gownes, and the 24{ty} put on their Gownes and then they goe and proclaime the fayre in 2 places, once against the Cock, and the other in the water fayre beyond the soapbarrells neere the Iron and next the River banke and soe goe againe to the Booth, and there at the dore of the booth is proclaymed the Court by the Serjeant Cryer, then in our Gownes the Mayor Aldermen and 24{ty} dyne, and after dinner all putt of their gownes and putt on their Cloakes, only Mr Mayor putts on his black Gowne and soe home againe, euery one leaving Mr Mayor according as the way to their homes leades.

Teusday about one in the afternoone began the sessions for the Towne I being with Mr Recorder Mr Spalding, Mr Moody and Mr Towne Clerke at Mr Mayors conferring about Towne busines, Mr Mayor would haue us all stay to dinner, wee had a giggott of boyled mutton caper sauce, 4 rabbetts in a dish, a dish of Hartechoakes, and 4 tarts of seuerall kindes in a dish and Claret immediately after dinner goeing home for our gownes wee went to the Hall and at the Sessions among other things Blackley a baker a priviledged person in the Vniuersity being bound ouer before for breach of the Peace by Mr Mayor appeared at the Sessions, pleading noe priviledge and paid the fees of the Court and was dismissed, seuerall Traverses tryed. The water Cocks or branches beyonnd the Conduit agreed and ordered to be seuered and cutt of *by or upon Munday the* 19 *July instant.*

Thirsday *Fryday* morning the Serjeant Tho. Harper came to mee to giue me notice that the Grand Common day was on Munday next in the afternoone at 1 of the Clock being the 17th [16th] day of Aug: (the proper day being the 16th [15th] day which this yeare fell on a Sunday) alsoe he gaue me notice from Mr Mayor, that I cause my apprentice to come in then to the Hall to be Registred if he expected any freedome.

Munday Grand Common day came in freeman *Alderman* Allens sonne a scholler in order to the taking upp his boothes. came in free alsoe Saml Newton my brother John Newtons sonne by his fathers coppy Jos: Pounsaby butcher late Treasurer for a fine of 10{li} passed offices; Mrs Chapman Widdow renewed a lease of a booth timber house at the ende of Barnewell for the terme of 21 yeares fine 10{s} Mr Stamford of Christs Colledge appointed Minister for the fayre: a Lease of some Almeshouses in Clement Parish sealed to Trustees there for the parish use, Norman the butcher paid in 3{li} for a fine

* Mr Crabb Mayor

Marginalia: 13 July Sessions; Mr Blackley baker bound ouer; Aug. 14 [13]; Aug. 17 [16]. Grand Common day for the renewing his lease of his slaughterhouse. a Committee appointed, of the Aldermen Mr Wilson Mr Moody Mr Adams and myselfe of the 24^{ty} Mayfeild &c. to veiw 2 houses to be granted by Lease the one at the Castle end, the other in Walls Lane called the shoulder of Mutton; Regulators appointed for the Fayre Mr Wilson Mr Moody Mr Adams and myselfe. *The* Mayor *that was* chosen for the ensueing yeare *was* Mr Philip Williams baker *Mayor*, Bayliffs More, Cooper, Eagle, Crosbey, Counsellors Alderman Herring   Coroners Mr Hawkins Tho. Flack. This day two Common Counsell men chose, Mr John Ilger in the roome of Mr Williamson deceased and John More in the roome of Mr Sedgewick who haueing not appeared at the Hall for the space of 2 yeares last past, they chose More in his roome Alderman Moody was much displeased he was not chose New Elect and said he would leaue the body because he was passed by: Mr New Elect made noe speech nor refusall but tooke his place and was sworne, and as wee were goeing into the Parlor the New Elect invited all to a glasse of wine in the Hall and soe all Aldermen and other Gownemen in the Parlor had 2 sugar cakes a peece and sack what was fit, as also Tobacco and small beere *and alsoe the freemen in the Hall seured* [?*stares*?]: and then the Company did rise and the Mayor New Elect &c. went away the New Elect took his leave of all at the Hall dore and the whole company went home with Mr Mayor and many went in and had strong beere and a dish of peares and soe parted. The Towne waytes alsoe played at the Hall after the eleccion was ouer. Middleton was alsoe propounded to goe out free by purchase but he did not. Fryday dyned at Mr Crabbs Mayor the Bayliffs and Treasurers with their wives.

20 Aug

20 Aug   Fryday Mr Williams new Elect, Mr Pettit, my selfe, Bird Alders and Blackerby veiwed and made report of the house at Castle End and Walls Lane.

23 Aug   *Munday Mr New Elect by the Serjeant invited all the Aldermen Bayliffs Treasurers and Attorneys to dyne with him at the Hall on Bartholomew day.*

* Mr Crabb Mayor

Tewsday Bartholomew day all the Aldermen in scarlett according to former notice went to the Hall, where they and all Gownemen at Mr New Elects charge had one cake and one glasse of sack a peece and from thence with Mr Recorder wee all tooke horse and went to Mr Mayors who being ready at his dore tooke horse alsoe and soe wee rode to proclaime the fayre, from whence being retourned to the Hall wee had the service of Cakes and wine of Mr Mayor and Mr New Elect who served alsoe the 24^{ty} and gownemen our service was from Mr Mayor 2 rolls 2 sugarcakes a peece and sack convenient and the like from the New Elect, after service of the wine and Cakes wee had a very good dinner in the Parlor at the long table where Mr Recorder alsoe dined vizt 2 dishes of boyled chickens, a line of veale, a legg of boyled mutton, 2 dishes of rosted neats tongues with udders venison sauce 2 exelent neats tongue pyes, a great peece of Rost beefe, 2 couple of capons, 2 couple of rost rabbetts 2 dishes of ducks one dish of patriges, 2 dishes of pidgeons and Tarts 4 in a dish and wine sack clarett and white plentifull, *alsoe in the 24^{ty} mans roome dined the Bayliffs and Treasurers new and old, the Attorneyes dyned in the Hall.* After dinner wee putt of our scarlet and putt on our black gownes, and then went to our Common Day busines, and there was granted to Waldgrave Kempe the renewall of his Lease *it being quite out* of a peece of ground next his roundabout in Garlick Row next Robin Hood to hold for 21 yeares rent 40^s per annum and for the fine of 20^s alsoe granted to Mr Tho. Buck for the fine of 5^{li} and the old rent and covenants the addicion of 4 yeares or thereabouts to make up his Lease 40 yeares of the ground and house in the occupacion of Jo Blackley in Slaughterhouse Lane being in St Edwards and Bennet parish in which Lease there is a Covenant to discharge the parish of St Edwards of all poore comeing to inhabit in the said house. The same day came in   Middleton butcher *freeman* for the fine of 5^{li}. The same day Mr Mayor propounded
Balls to come in his freeman which was granted, the same day granted to Sanders *blacksmith* at Castle End the house

24 Aug Grand Common day

there in his use for 21 yeares for the fine of 5^{li}. The same
day granted to the wife and childe of Saml Gray chandler the
Shoulder of Mutton in Walls Lane for 21 yeares for the fine
of 20^{li}. The same day granted to Mr Mayor 12^{li} odd money
by him laid out for the Towne. The same day the Regulators for the fayre received their Letter of Attorney from
the Towne under seale. *The same day the 100^{li} that M^r
Chapman gave was taken out of the chest and delivered to
Mr Mayor to be lent vnto Clare Hall under their Colledge
seale, till we could heare of a purchase to lay it out upon.*

Sept dyed at Impington Mr Tho. Whybrow Vicar there and buryed.

Sept dyed Saml Rix brewer.

28 Sept Tewsday morning Tom Harper came to mee in Mr Mayor
and Mr New Elects name to desire mee to be at the Hall tomorrow morning *about 8 of the clock* being Michaelmas day

29 Sept
Mr Philip
Williams
Mayor
to accompany them to Trinity Church. Wednesday Michaelmas day All went to the Towne Hall and from thence
with Mr Mayor and Mr New Elect to Trinity Church where
after service Mr Neach of Pembroke Hall preached on the
13 Romans 1. Let every soule be subject &c. from thence all
went to the Hall, and being in the Parlor considering what
was fit to be propounded went into the Hall and after that
was done, Mr Crab made a speech, to this effect, that he
was glad he had finished his yeare and was glad if any service
he had done the Towne was acceptable &c. Then was M^r
Williams sworne Mayor with the other officers, then was
sent a Bayliffe for the Vice Chancellor who with some doctors and the Proctors swore the Mayor not to enfringe the
lawfull libertyes of the University, then the Vicechancellor &c. departed without any invitacion or soe much as a
glasse of wine, then wee went into the Parlor till dinner
ready, there dyned strangers Lord Allington and his brother
Lord Wootton, Sir Tho Sclater, Dr Stoyt, Do^r Fayrebrother,
Captain Story, Captain Milleson, Walter Pratt, Mr Neach,
Vincent, Herring (?) and the Curat of Trinity, after dinner
cloath taken away and hands washt, was laid a cleane cloath

and a banquet in voydors, and afterwards all went to Mr Mayors and had 2 sugar cakes and 2 roles, and sack and from thence all but Mr Mayor went to Mr Crabbs and there had 2 sugar cakes 2 rolls and sack and soe away home. Saturday morning *betweene 7 and 8 of the clock* dyed Francis Hughes Esquire Beadle of the Vniversity of Cambridge, he dyed at his lodgeings in Trinity Hall; he made and sealed his will dated the 21st October 1669, he was buryed in St Buttolphs Church on All Saints evening *being the 1st November* 1669.

30th October. Mr Hughes dyed

Tewsday came in Lewis Covile baker free man and passed then offices all for the fine of 5ll; Mr Matthew Blackley paid his fine of, 40s to the Towne for refusing and passing the office of Treasurer, William Hurry for the fine of 20s passed his office of Treasurer, Mr Samuell Moodey under his hand sent to Mr Mayor at the Common day in the Hall his resignacion of his Aldermans place. *A man betweene *Lowleworth and the Hills in Huntingdon*[1] *rode* was robbed (as was supposed by 2 schollers one of Sydney and the other of Emmanuel) of 6ll*.

Common day. Nov. 2 Mr Moodey resigned his Aldermans place

Nov. 2

was chose Mr Peck of St Johns Colledge one of the Esquire Beadles in the roome of Mr Hughes deceased.

2nd Novr. Mr Peck chose Beadle

Thirsday in the afternoone in a full Congregacion at the Consistory was chosen James Duport (Master of Magdalen College in Cambridge) Vicechancellour of the Vniuersity of Cambridge.

4 Nov.

Munday at a meeting of the Master and Seniors of Trinity Colledge in Cambridge in the Lodgeing of the Master I was propounded and partly then concluded that I should be Auditor of Trinity Colledge. On Thirsday morning the 11th Nov. 1669 at a meeting in the Chappell by the Master and Seniors (as I was informed according to the usage in such cases) an oath was given to the seniors that they did beleiue

Nov 8

* Mr Philip Williams Mayer

[1] The words "Girton and Hokeington (?)" were written first and then replaced by the words in italics.

me to be a fitt person to be Auditor, and thereupon it was there in the chappell concluded and agreed that I should be the Colledge Auditor, when it was concluded Do[r] Crane my very great friend in that busines (as was the Master and all the Seniors) came to me towards the lower end of the chappell and wished me joy in my Auditors place, soone after the Master (being Do[r] John Pearson) called mee to him and tould mee that he and the Seniors had chosen mee to be the Colledge Auditor, for which I retourned my humble thankes to them all; (present then Do[r] Pearson Master; Do[r] Chamberlaine Vicemaster, M[r] Nevile, Do[r] Marshall, M[r] Bayley, Do[r] Crane, M[r] Lynnet, M[r] Scott and M[r] Stedman.) The next day being fryday according to the Statutes of the Colledge I was in the Chappell, in my gowne sworne to the said Office for my faithfull discharge of it according to the statutes of the Colledge and of the Founder; the oath is in the 11th chapter of the statutes, and the Statute appointing the Auditor is the 36th Statute, soe when I was sworne: I wrote by their appointment in a folio booke covered with leather wherein the officers of the Colledge at their eleccion and being sworne, write their names and the office to which they were elected. That which I writt with my owne hand was this 12° Novemb. 1669 Sam[l] Newton Auditor juratus.

12 Nov. Fryday Sam[l]. Newton auditor juratus Coll. Trin.

The yearly allowance from Trinity Colledge to the Auditor as is entered in the senior Bursars yeares booke *in the Title of Patents and Fees* is as followeth viz.

	li.	s.	d.	li.	s.	d.
To the Auditor his fee	5	0	0			
To him for engrossing the Audit Rolls	6	13	4	16	0	0
To him for his Augmentacion	3	6	8			
To him for his Arrearage bookes	1	0	0			

More entered in the yeare booke of M[r] Benjamin Pulleyn Junior Bursar 1669 under the Title of Extraordinaryes

	li.	s.	d.
To the Auditor for billets	0	6	8

More entered in the yearebooke 1669 of Mr William Corker Steward under the title of The Audit Bills

To the Auditor for pens inke and paper and for his man . 1 2 8

and more there under the title of Extraordinaryes:

To the Auditor for a warp of Lyng at Stirbridge fayre . 0 6 8

More from John Stagg Manciple in Kinde,

A Coller of brawne,
Alsoe a dish of wild fowle, or 6 8

Alsoe from the Brewhouse 2 barrels of strong beere *one in March and the other in September.*

Wednesday betweene 11 and 12 at night Anne Mathewes the wife of W^m. Mathewes shoomaker (then lyeing sick of the small pox within an houre or two after her deliuery of a daughter borne aliue) dyed and was buried on Thirsday night the 16th Decr. 1669 *and her daughter which was alsoe named Anne dyed on Fryday morning the* 17 Dec. 1669.

15 December Anne Mathewes dyed

Thirsday night about 7 of the clock dyed Alderman Samuel Spaldyng.

16th Dec. Alderman Spaldyng dyed

Saturday about 8 of the clock in the forenoone dyed Mr Thomas Gibbs a devout charitable pious man *a patterne of piety and patience.* He was conduct of Trinity Colledge and Minister of G^t St Maryes Parish in Cambridge and was about the age of 76 yeares when he dyed and was buryed on Sunday night following the 19th Decr. 1669 in Trinity Colledge Chappell.

18th December Mr Gibbs dyed

Fryday on or about this day dyed the Right Noble George (Monke) Duke of Albemarle.

31 Decem. Ld Monke dyed

[16$\frac{69}{70}$]

Tewsday next after Twelfe being a Grand Common day, their being 2 Aldermen to be chosen, the one in the roome of Alderman Saml Moodey by reason of his resigneing of his Aldermans place the last Common Day, and the other

11 Jan. Owen Mayfeild Edward Lawe chose Aldermen

* Mr Philip Williams Maior

in the roome of Alderman Saml Spaldyng lately deceased, First in the roome of Alderman Moodey was chosen Owen Mayfeild Vintner who accepted thereof, and then after Mr Mayor had declared him and he had accepted, the 24^{ty} went to fill up their number, and in the roome of Mr Mayfield, they chose Edward Lawe Towne Clerke to be one of the 24^{ty} who accepted thereof, and afterwards in the Parlor the Aldermen chose the said Edward Lawe Alderman in the roome of Mr Spalding, who within 3 dayes after declared his acceptance thereof.

12 Feb
John
Smith
dyed

Saturday in the afternoone dyed John Smith of Bennet parish shoemaker one of the 24^{ty}.

4 March
Mr Tho.
Buck
Beadle
dyed

Fryday about 9 at night dyed Thomas Buck Esquire Beadle at his house in St Edwards parish in Cambridge, the bell rang not for him till next morning, and he was buryed in the north chancell of St Edwards church in Cambridge in the upper north corner on Munday the 7th March 1669.

March 7

Munday at the consistory were pricked for Beadle (in the roome of Mr Thomas Buck) Mr Wm Worts of Cajus College and Vrlyne of Pembroke Hall.

March 8th

Tewsday at the Consistory at a full Congregacion there betweene 9 and eleaven in the morning was chosen elected

Mr Worts
chosen
Beadle

and sworne *William* Worts Master of Arts and Fellow of Gonvile and Cajus Colledge in Cambridge, one of the Esquire Beadles of the Vniversity of Cambridge, in the roome and place of Mr Thomas Buck Esquire Beadle deceased. Mr Vrlyn stood against him and was prickt with him but lost it by 16 votes; there being for Mr Worts 108 and for Mr Vrlyn but 92.

[1670]

Aprill 17

Sunday about 3 of the Clock in the afternoone dyed my brother in law Mr John Cole at Sutton in the Isle of Ely.

Aprill
Old M^{rs}
Spalding
dyed

Saturday in the morning betweene 2 and 3 of the clock

* Mr Philip Williams Maior

dyed Mrs Elizabeth Spaldyng widdow the Relict of Alderman Saml Spaldyng deceased.

dyed Susanna the wife of my cosin Philip Welbore. *Apr. My cosin Welbores wife dyed*

Tewsday at a Grand Common day after proposicions made in the Hall about the renewall of Leases and other businesses which are first dispatcht, then they went to the eleccion of Mayor Bayliffs and Coroners and other officers for the ensueing yeare, and they elected Alderman Edward Lawe (who was then Towne Clerke) to be New Elect or Mayor for the ensueing yeare, who sayd to the House, Gentlemen there are seuerall subject to your eleccion which are more fitt for this place and I wish you had made choice of some of them; soe he presently tooke his place, and said Gentlemen I desire you to drinke a glasse of wine with mee at my house and soone after all went (*Mayor* Aldermen 24{ty} and freemen) along with him to his house, where first were served to euery man 2 rolls and 2 sugarcakes, and then they had sack and clarett for the space of an houre what they would drinke, *Mrs *New Elect appeared not** and then departed without sight of Mrs New Elect. *The Towne waytes played at the House all the while.* *Aug. 16. Grand Common day*

Tewsday morning betweene the houres of 9 and 10 were marryed by Mr Serjeant minister of St Edwards parish in Cambridge in Kings Colledge Chappell by and with the leave and consent (being requested by mee) of the Provost, Thomas Watson of Ely draper and Margaret Cole of Sutton in the Isle of Ely widdow. *September 27th Sister Cole marryed to Mr Watson*

Thirsday. At a Grand Common day, after Mr Williams (the old Mayor) declared that he had now finished his yeare and was obliged to the house for their assisting him, Mr Edward Lawe was sworne maior, the same day came in Sir Thomas Sclater Baronett freeman and was sworne soe. *Sept. 29. Mr Law sworne maior and Sr. Thos. Sclater Freeman*

Saturday betweene 4 and 5 in the afternoone came to Towne the Duke of York and his Dutchess and the Dutchess of Cleaveland the major Aldermen and 24 gownemen met them *Oct. 2 Duke and Dutchess of Yorke came to Cambridge*

* Mr Philip Williams Mr Edward Lawe Maior

all 3 in one coach against New England they went away from hence to Newmarket Sunday in the afternoone.

<small>Oct. 2
Mr Lee dyed</small>

Sunday morning dyed Mr John Lee Cooke of Kings Colledge and buryed on Tewsday night at Great St Maryes Church.

<small>Nov. 26th The Prince of Orange his Reception</small>

Saturday morning about 10 of the Clock came in to Cambridge his Highnesse the Prince of Orange being then betweene 19 and 20 yeares of age a well Countenanced man a smooth and smeeger face and a hansome head of hayre of his owne, there were in all 3 Coaches 6 horses a peece, the Prince was in the middlemost, and sat at the head end thereof on the right hand, the Lord Ossery sat in the same end with him, Mr Law then Mayor being then at London Mr Herring was his deputy who with the Aldermen in scarlett, and the Common Counsell and other Gownemen in their habitts being ready at the Dolphin Inne, mett and saluted the Prince at the hither end of Jesus Lane against the Dolphin, just upon the Turne of his Coach, and Mr Herring did present himselfe to him, who in a Courteous manner leaned over my Lord Ossery and gave audience to the Deputy Mayor who made there a short speech, the substance whereof was, that hee was there to wayt upon his Highnesse and to assure him of his hearty wellcome to the Towne, and should be most ready to doe him all *becoming* service *that was in our power*, and thought it his duty at that time to pay the *due* respects of his Majesties subjects of this Towne unto his Highnesse and wished that his stay might haue bin longer amongst us, that wee might have had a better opportunity of evidencing that respects and service which was due unto him, but did assure him that wee were and would remayne *in all offices* his most obedient servants and therewith made a low obedience to the Prince, the Prince retourned him thankes for the respects, and said he had a minde to see this Towne but his busines was such as would permitt but a short stay, otherwise he would have gratifyed our desires with his company longer and then after due respects on each side,

* Mr Law Mayor

the Coaches passed on downe by St Johns to the Schooles, where there was a Comencement for severall degrees at which time many went out Doctors and masters of Arts but not perfect in their degrees till Munday after *because the Prince could not stay* at which time my cosin William Ellis went out master of Arts *and was perfected and created as to his degree on Munday the 28th Nov.* 1670. The Prince and his retinue dyned at the Provosts of Kings Colledge and after dinner went to Trinity Colledge and soe went the same night to Audle end, and the next day to London. One Mr Samburne deputed master of the Ceremonyes was with Mr Mayor upon his first saluting the Prince and directed him how he might know the Prince, and ordered the Coaches to stand still till Mr Mayor had delivered his speach.

My cosin William Ellis tooke his master of Arts degree at Cambridge 28 Nov. 1670 when the Prince of Orange was heere.

[167¾]

Tewsday at a generall Common day adjorned from the Tewsday before to this day, was the Patent of Sir Thomas Chicheley sealed for his being High Steward of Cambridge. The same day came in and were sworne Freeman Captain Hunt and Mr Turner at the Rose, Mr Turner came in Mr Mayors Freeman, and both then past offices given them by consent of the House; they both together gave a Treat of wine at the Rose to the Mayor Aldermen and 24ty &c.

17th Jan.

High Steward

Captain Hunt Mr Turner freemen

Wednesday morning about 6 of the Clock *being St Paul's day* departed this life Bridget Incarsole the wife of John Incarsole, formerly before her marriage her name was Bridget Raymond.

25 January Bridget Incarsole dyed.

Saturday morning *about 5 of the Clock* dyed Mrs Mary Bainbrigg widdow the Relict of Dr Bainbrigg late Master of Christs Colledge in Cambridge, *and shee was buryed in St Edwards Chancel on Tewsday night between 8 and 9 of the Clock.*

25 Febr. Mrs Bainbrig dyed.

* Thirsday came to Board with mee John Welbore and Philip Welbore, sonnes of my cosin Philip Welbore of Foxton, my Cosin Welbore is by agreement that I made with him

2 March My cosin Welbores children come to board.

* Mr Law Mayor

to allow mee for their Board at and after the rate of 20ᵘ, per Annum and in case of their extraordinary sicknes, as the small pox or the like, my cosin Welbore is to bee at the sole charge of such sicknes, and of a Nurse if occasion bee.*

[1671]

May 5th

Sessions

Fryday was the Sessions held in and for the Towne of Cambridge. Mʳ Recorder was absent he being gone (as it was said) to the Bath concerning his Lamenes. Councellor Halman sat in the Recorders Roome and gave the Charge.

May 11th
Duke of Buckingham Lᵈ. Chancelor

Thirsday the Vniuersity at a meeting in the Consistory or Regent House elected for their Lord Chancelour George Duke of Buckingham, in the Roome of Edward Earle of Manchester lately deceased.

May 9th
Kings Crowne stole

Tewsday the Kings Crowne Scpter and Globe was by 5 Rogues stolen and taken away out of the place in the Tower where they are kept, 2 of them escaped out of the Tower, before they were discouered the other 3 were taken before they got out *or gott away from* of * the Tower and with them were taken the Crowne septer and globe. The Rogues went under pretence as strangers to see those Rarityes, and when they were in the Roome with him, that was to shew them, they bound and gagg'd him but the rogues being gone out of the roome, he made a noyse that a Centenal neere there heard, who presently came and understanding the matter presently went after them and tooke 3 of the rogues before they got out of the Tower one being in a Parsons habit.

26 May

Easter Paving Leet

Dʳ Bretton of Emm: Col Vice Chancʳ.

Fryday in the forenoone about 10 of the Clock (Mʳ Hering being deputy Mayor) according to Notice from him by the Serjeant I went to Sᵗ Maryes Magna in my Gowne, where was the Vice Chancelor and Proctors and Dʳ King and Mʳ Mayor and Alderman Finch, Alderman Muryell and James Alders and John Ilger and the Bayliffs Eagle and Crosley, there was alsoe Mʳ Whyn and Mʳ Sell, the busines was to swear the paving Leet, the Jury being called 12 by Mʳ Whyn and 12 by Mʳ Sell, Mʳ Whyn swore them to make

* Mr Lawe Mayor

true presentment and then read their charge out of a book; and afterwards the Vice Chancellor spoke to them in this sort What has bin declared to you in your charge you are strictly and duely to observe as well for that it is not onely for the generall good both of Vniuersity and Town but to every one of you in particuler it is a conveniency and benefit, for the decency and cleanlynes of the streets is as well pleasurable as tending to health, and when you doe herein act for the publique welfare of both bodyes you do in particuler act for your selves. I shall not need to say anything of your oath which you have taken how much it doth oblige you, *a bare* he that will not perform his beare promise made, is counted a very unworthy person, an Oath is a religious promise that bindes to God, and has bin in that case given you for the more strict observance of your duty in a matter that Law and custome has thought fitt to enjoyne upon you and therefore you ought to be the more conscious in your performance thereof.

Then the Vice Chancellor asked Mr Mayor when it would be convenient for the Jury to give in their verdict, and Mr Mayor tould the Vice Chancellor if he pleased on Tewsday next in the morning and Order accordingly was given them, then Mr Sell the deputy Towne Clerke askt Mr Mayor what fine should be imposed on such as made default in appearance and M^r amerced them 3^s 4^d a peice and soe Mr Vice Chancellor tooke his leave of Mr Mayor and went away, and then Mr Mayor went away, the Aldermen all going to their own homes.

Teusday about   in the evening dyed Richard Pyke sonne of Ric. Pyke. *20 June Ric. Pyke*

Thursday the Mayor and Aldermen proclaymed Midsommer fayre, wee all went to Mr Mayors house between 8 and 9 in the morning and there had a glasse of sack and every one a sugarcake and soe Mr Mayor in his scarlett and the Aldermen in their Cloakes and Coates went to the fayre but there put on their Scarlet gownes and the Common Councell their gownes. *22nd June Midsommer fayre.*

22th June   Thursday morning was marryed in S. Edwards Church in Cambridge John Cranway to   Nicholson the daughter of Mr Thomas Nicholson.

(All Generall Common dayes Notice is given thereof 2 days before.)

16 Aug.
S. N. New Elect

Wednesday at a Generall Common Day I S. N. was chosen New Elect on the same day Alderman Edward Wilson by a writing dated the 16 Aug. 1671 did resigne up his place of an Alderman into the hands of the Mayor and Aldermen and did thereby auctorize them to choose another in his roome. There was then chosen preacher for the fayre Mr More of Clare Hall.

The expence at this day

Wine 18 q^{ts}. of sack and 6 of Claret	2 . 5 . 0
19^{ll}. of Cakes	0 . 19 . 0
G^t. St M. Bells	0 . 5 . 0
S^t. Edw. Bells	0 . 2 . 6
Waytes	0 . 10 . 0
Tobacco	0 . 2 . 0
	4 . 3 . 6

22 Aug
Assizes.
Judges visit.

Tewsday Assizes, according to notice the Aldermen met at Mr Mayors where was alsoe the Recorder, wee had neither wine nor beere there, from thence we went to salute the Judges, which were Judge Hales and Judge Turner. Mr Recorder sayd little onely desired his execuse from his *owne and our* attendance at the Assizes, neither Mr Mayor nor any other said anything *......* and each of the Judges *...* *gave us their respects* and soe we departed. Onely it seemes it is usuall for the Mayor if the Recorder be not there present, to desire the Judges to execuse *the* *our* attendance at the Castle, for it seemes *they* the Mayor and Aldermen are to give their attendance there on the Judges, and noat that the New Elect and not the Recorder goes next the Mayor.

* Mr Lawe Maior

I gave the Mayor, Aldermen, Common Councell, Bayliffs new and old, Treasurers new and old and Attorneyes a dinner at my owne house. 24 Aug.

Fryday in the afternoon dyed Old Mrs Crabb the mother of Alderman Crabb. Septemb. 1st. Old M^{rs}. Crabb dyed

I sent to Dr Mapletoft Master of Pembroke Hall or in his absence to the President there to provide one to preach the Sermon on Michaelmas Day, the New Elect being to give him notice. 20 Sept.

Tewsday Mr Mayor called us to a meeting to acquaint us that his majestie King Charles the 2nd would come to Cambridge on Wednesday the 4th October next. At the same time wee agreed that Mr Muryell should goe to London to Sir Thomas Chicheley our High Steward to advise about the present and if he thought fit then six score peeces of *brought* *broad* gold to be presented to the King and if the Queene came with him shee to be presented with 100 guynyes. 19 Sept.

Michaelmas day at 8 in the morning all met at the Hall and from thence went to Trinity Church where preached Mr Vrlin on these words on the 5th of Matthew Christ came not to brake but to fullfill the Law, the cheife of his discourse was concerning the obedience due unto Magistracy. after sermon wee went all in order to the Hall, and there at the Common day I was sworne Mayor and tooke the oathes as in such cases and the Vice Chancellor and Proctors Dr Bretton of Emmanuel College Vice Chancellor came and gaue mee their Oath, then the rest of the Officers sworne then Mr Lawe the old Maior tould them Gentlemen I have now finished my yeare and have therein indeavored as much as in mee lay to continue peace amongst you and am obliged to you all for your ready assistance at all times, and I doubt not but the gentleman that succeeds will haue as due a care in his place. And thereupon I made a short speech signifyeing to them How that in my owne sense I was a very unmeet person for soe weighty a place yet that the utmost of my care 29 Sept. Saml Newton Maior should not be wanting for the due discharge thereof not doubting of their good and ready assistance to mee &c. Then I tooke the Chayre or place of Maioralty, After that at the same Common Day I propounded Hildebrand Allington Esquire, brother to my Lord Allington, Sir Thomas Hatton and Talbot Pepys sonne of our Recorder to haue the freedome of the Towne, and it was granted them gratis, they gaue to the poore mans box, and they were sworne then freemen. Then I adjoined the Common Day till Munday following to 2 of the clock being the 2^d Oct., and soe wee went into the Parlor and stayed till dinner without sack or any beere, and then came to dinner in the Hall, the old Mayor sat next me and I carved *all* *most*. After dinner wee went into the Parlor and dranke a tankard of ale, and then my Lord Allington and all the strangers and company went with mee home to my house, where they had each of them 2 sugar cakes and 2 rolls, (*as the manner usually is*) and wine what they pleased. And then the whole company accompanyed Mr Law the old Mayor home, and had a service of wine and cake there, and then went home, Robert Drake attorney was chosen one of the 24^{ty} this day.

30 Sept.

Saturday I Saml Newton was by virtue of a commission directed to Mr Herring, Mr Law and others sworne (before Mr Hering and Mr Law) one of his Majesties Justices of the Peace of the Towne of Cambridge.

Oct 4. King Charles the 2nd his comeing to Cambridge

Wednesday being a very cleere sunshiney day, his Majestie King Charles the 2nd came to Cambridge *the* 1st *time*. The place in which the Corperacion mett him was on Christs Colledge peece, on the Greene sword to which place the Mayor Recorder Aldermen and all Gownemen repayred the Mayor and Aldermen *in Scarlet* on horseback all the rest of the Gownemen on foot, the *Maior and* Aldermen *alight there and* had there matts to kneele on, it was about 10 of the clock *or between* 10 *and* 11 in the morning his Majestie came thither, he came in his coach and with him therein, the Earle of Suffolk and my Lord Allington of Horsehcath

* Saml Newton Maior

he did not there alight out of his coach, when he came at us, his coach stood, And I having the Mace then ready in my hand I spake these words upon my knees unto his Majestie

May it please your most Exellent Majestie According to my bounden duty I doe in all humility resigne up this into your sacred hands as your just right. And therewithall upon my knees tendred his Majestie my mace, who strecht out his hand and toucht it and retourned it to mee againe; Then did our Recorder Peapys make a short speech, and then at such time as he spoke of the present I stept forward to his Majesties Coach and upon my knee presented the same into the hands of his Majestie who tooke it and layd it in his lapp, the present was 100 twenty shilling peeces of broad gold in a crimson coullered velvet or good plush purse with gold fringe and gold strings.

After Mr Recorders speech was ended, his Majestie gave mee out his hand to kisse, soe upon my knee I tooke his Majestie by the hand (as the manner is) and kissed it.

Then he held out his hand to the Recorder to kisse, who kissed it, and then the Aldermen kist the Kings hand. his Majestie came not out of the Coach. Then all the Common Counsell and gownemen went 2 and 2 *first* in order the Juniors first, then the Aldermen on horseback in scarlett 2 and 2 in rank the Juniors first, then the Kettle Drum on horseback, then his Majesties Trumpeters 4 or 6 of them, then I as Mayor on horseback with the Towne Mace in my hand betweene two of his Majestie's Macebearers *with their two Maces, each of which 2 maces was much bigger than our biggest Towne mace* then followed his Majesties Coach in which he was; then his Majesties lifeguard, then the Towne souldiers; all of us except the souldiers were beare headed, soe wee waited on his Majestie as far as the Regent Walke where he was received by the Vniuersity, then I and the Aldermen went to the Towne Hall where wee had a very plentifull dinner at which were most of the Knights and Gentlemen of the Country, and dyned there alsoe my Lord Allington and Sir Thomas Chicheley the former is our Burgesse for Parliament the latter our High Steward. The Conduit run claret wine when his Majestie passed by who was well pleased with it. *Sir Thomas Chicheley was pleased to come downe from London on purpose the better to Countenance us, in our appearance, Major Harsenet one of His Majesties Serjeants at Mace lodged at my House the same time and continued there severall nights, His Majestie retourned from Cambridge to Newmarket the same Wednesday.*

My feast at Christmas 1671

<small>Presents sent mee in</small>

Mʳ Jacob 6 bottles of sack and a sugarloafe
Mʳˢ Sarah Simpson widdow a Cagg of Sturgeon
Mʳ Wᵐ Hinton a Cagg of Sturgeon and 6 bottles of Wine
Mʳ   Turner at the Rose a Cagg of Sturgeon
Alderman Herring 2 geese one Cock Turkey and Pottatoes
Alderman Tifford one whole sheep
Alderman Pettit 2 Turkeyes and 6 bottles of Wine
Alderman Crabb one Turkey 6 mallard and some other Wildefowle
Alderman Muriell a Coller of Brawne and one Turkey
Alderman Law 12 bottles of sack and 6 of Clarett
Alderman Adams 6 bottles of sack and 6 of Clarett
Alderman Williams 5 bottles of sack and 5 of Clarett
Alderman Mayfeild a large * peece * *joll* of Sturgeon and 6 bottles of sack and 6 bottles of clarett
Mʳ Blackerly a little * peece * *Gowle* of Sturgeon
Alderman Cropley sent noe present
Alderman Finch was then lately dead
Mʳ Hawkins a Turkey and 2 joints of Porke
Mʳ Alders 6 Tapers or mould Candles
Mʳ Robson a Coller of Brawne and 6 bottles of sack and 6 of Claret
Mʳ Bird a dish of fish

The Bayliffes 12 bottles of sack and 12 of Claret
The Treasurers 6 bottles of sack and 6 of Clarett

Mʳ Pyke Attorney 10 bottles of Clarett

Mr Baron 10 bottles of Caret
Mr Sell 10 bottles of Claret
Mr Fox 2 Turkeyes Attorney
Mr Drake 6 bottles of sack and 6 of Clarret
Mr Jermyn a dish of Fish
Mr Fox the Common Counsell a Coller of Brawne
Mr Walker a Chine of Mutton and Chine of Veale
Mr Robson as Common Counsell 10 bottles of Claret
Mr Felsted 9 bottles of Clarrett
Mr More 9 bottles of Clarrett
Mr More at the workhouse 4 bottles of sack and a Turkey
Mr Crabb the Toller 2 Turkeyes

[1672]

I received for my selfe on this day *being Thirsday* at the first Port for my part cleere and all fees and all owances paid and made 13^{li} 6^s 8^d that is to say for my dividend 7^{li} 7^s 0^d and from the 4 Serjeants out of their bayles and withdraughts 5^{li} 19^s 8^d. Memorandum I gave the Serjeants out of what they paid me 4^s a peice but the said 13^{li} 6^s 8^d I had over and above and besides 1^{li} 6^s 8^d allowed towards the port supper. *(9 May 1st Port)*

Saturday morning dyed Robert Eade Doctor in Physick. *(11 May Dr Eade dyed)*

Wednesday in the afternoone dyed Mrs Bodenham Dr Wigmores daughter the wife of Beaumont Bodenham Esqre *shee was buryed on Thursday night the 11th July 1672 at St Edwards Church in Cambridge.* *(10 July)*

Was elected Alderman Owen Mayfeild to be Maior for the ensueing yeare. *(16 Aug)*

Sunday *The Mayor and* All The Aldermen in their Scarlett, and the Common Councell and Bayliffes in their Gownes at 8 of the Clock mett at the Hall and from thence went to St Edwards Church, and from thence to the Hall and being a little while in the Parlor, wee came out and went upon the Bench, and there I rose up and spake as followeth vizt The busines of this day at this time in this *(29th Sept S. N. upon his giveing up his place of Maioralty)*

5—2

place is very well knowne to all heere present. And now Gentlemen I haue ended my yeare, And how much the honour and reputacion of this Corporacion hath suffered under the weake mannagement of soe unworthy an Instrument as my selfe is, I now am and allwayes have bin sufficiently sencible, In this matter I begg your excuse and pardon, But Gentlemen give me leave to tell you, That I was never able to doe anything for you, but I was ready willing and dilligent to doe it to the utmost of my power, I have allwayes endeavoured to mainteine peace and love *with* *amongst* you, and I hope I leave you fast tyed in the bands of amity and friendshipp free from Contencion. There Remaines therefore now noe more for mee to doe *but* onely to retourne you my thankes (which I heartily doe) for that Countenance favour and assistance I have had from you in the execucion of my Office, what has bin wanting in mee I doubt not wilbe amply supplyed by the care and diligence of this worthy Gentleman that is to succeed mee, to whome I wish all honour respects and good successe, And soe I humbly take my leaue of you and resigne upp my Office and place to be conferred as by Law and custome it ought to bee. And thereupon I gaue my place to M[r] Alderman Mayfeild who was immediately sworne but he made noe speach nor said anything.

After all things done at the Hall and the Common day continued till Tewsday following all the Aldermen and Common Councell went home with the Mayor, but the Aldermen onely dyned with him, and after dinner wee all went to S[t] Maryes to Church and then retourned home with the Mayor to his dore and there left him, Alderman Pettit, Alderman Williams, Alderman Robson came home with mee and 2 of the Bayliffes M[r] Crosby and M[r] Saunders and we drank a glasse of wine there at my house and soe they left mee.

On the Tewsday following betweene 8 and 9 in the morning wee all met at the Hall in our Scarlett &c. and from thence went to S[t] Edwards and after Sermon retourned in our Orders to the Hall where wee dyned and after dinner wee all went home with Mr Mayor where wee had Cakes and wine, and afterwards the whole Company strangers and others came home with mee to my house as namely the Earle of Sandwich his 2 sonnes then of Trinity Colledge Mr North my Lord Norths sonne Sir Thomas Sclater Sir Levinus Bennet Sir Thomas Wendy the Provost of Kings Colledge the Proctors and severall others with the Aldermen Common Counsell Bayliffs Freemen where I treated them with wine and Cakes which cost mee at that time above 5^{li} and soe they friendly departed.

[167$\frac{2}{3}$]

At a grand Common Day was Alderman Pettits resignacion published in the Hall and the same Day was chose in his Roome Mr Andrew Hart of the Common Counsell to be Alderman who being then gone for London, the Common Day was putt off to the Munday following for his acceptance or refusall *on which Munday he appeared, declared his acceptance and tooke his place on the Bench.* Tewsday 7th Jan Mr Hart chose Alderman

Mr Richard Pettit late Alderman, dyed in the afternoone of the same day *betweene 3 and 4 of the clock* and buryed in St Edwards *Churchyard at the end of the Steeple* on Sunday following in the afternoone being the 12th January 1672. *Mr Hughes our Minister preached his funerall sermon on these words in the 25 Matthew the last verse But the righteous into eternal life.* Fryday the 16th January Mr Alderman Pettit dyed

In the morning Doctor Mapletoft Master of Pembroke Hall sent for mee, and acquainted mee that hee with the rest of the Fellowes concerned had chosen mee to bee their Register of the said Colledge in the roome of Alderman Pettit deceased. Thirsday the 16th January S. N. chose Register of Pembrooke Hall

Sunday my cosin Susannah Ellis marryed to Mr Owen Jones at Waddesdon. January 19 Cosin Su. Ellis marryed

* Mr Owen Mayfield Maior.

Jan 26 Wm Mathewes marryed	Sunday William Mathewes Cordwayner marryed to Margaret Mortlock at Pampisford.
Feb^r the 6th Mrs Sheward dyed	Thirsday night dyed Mrs Katherine Sheward Widdow.
Feb. 7 Mrs Dickenson dyed	Fryday in the forenoone dyed Mrs Dickenson Mr Woottons daughter of Malton, the wife Mr Dickenson bookseller.
Febr. 9th Dr Pearson consecrated B^p of Chester	Sunday John Pearson Doctor in Divinity and Master of Trinity Colledge in Cambridge was consecrated Bishopp of Chester.
15 14th February Dr Crane dyed	*Saturday* *Fryday* morning dyed at London Dr Robert Crane, one of the Senior Fellowes of Trinity Colledge in Cambridge.
Feb. 24th Mr Stedman Senr fell. of Tr. Coll.	On Monday St Mathias day Mr Stedman was chose one of the Seniors of Trinity Colledge upon the death of Dr Crane.
27th Febr. Dr Isaac Barrow Master of Trin. Coll.	Thirsday in the afternoone came Dr Isaac Barrow Master of Trinity Colledge, the first time it was that he came after the Mastershipp was given him by the King, *he came then from London.*
5th March Dr Paman Vniuersity orator	Wednesday morning Dr Paman of St Johns College chose the Vniuersity Oratour in the roome of Dr Withrington who resigned that Office upon his being chosed Margarett Professor of Divinity for the Vniuersity *in the roome of Dr Bishop Pearson.*

[1673]

31 May Mrs Anne Baron	On Saturday came Mrs Anne Baron to board with mee *Mr Baron the 6. Sept. 1673 paid me 4^{li} for his daughters board for a quarter ending the last day of August 1673 and paid mee alsoe afterwards what was due for her board.*

* Mr Owen Mayfield Mayor.

Owen Hamond Draper marryed to Susannah Rix the widdow of Saml Rix brewer deceased on Thirsday the 28th day of August 1673 at Duxford.

Mr Owen Hamond marryed

[167¾*]

Thirsday at the County Court was Sir Thomas Hatton Knight and Baronet chose Knight of the Sheire for this County to sitt in Parliament in the Roome of Sir Thomas Wendy Knight of the Bath lately deceased, there stood against him   Russell Esquire of Fordham and Wren Esquire

January the 15th

Knight of the Sheir

All the said 3 had there men pol'd and sworne Sir Thomas Hatton had 872: Mr Russell had 823: and Mr Wren had 557: soe Sir Thomas Hatton carryed it by 49 votes. *They were poleing till Fryday night.*

Tewsday being a frosty morning, In the afternoone about 4 of the Clock it thundred prety loud two severall times.

17th Feb. Thunder

Mr Thomas Griffith of Trinity Colledge in Cambridge dyed on Saturday morning at London the 21th March 1673 *about 3 of the Clock.*

Mr Griffith dyed

being Munday in the morning I Samuell Newton and my cosin William Ellis were by the Master and Seniors of Trinity Colledge chose into the Office of Register of the same Colledge then vacant by the death of the said Mr Griffith To hold and enjoy the said office or place of Register unto the said Samuel Newton and William Ellis, soe that if there be a fayler by death or otherwise in either then the other to succeed in the said place.

23th March Trinity Colledge Register chose

On Munday after chappell in the afternoone was done wee the said Samuel Newton and William Ellis were sworne in the Chappell of the said Colledge, into the Office of Auditor of the said Colledge, which Office was confirmed unto us by Patent under the Colledge seale bearing date the 23th March 1673.

23 March Auditor of Tr: Coll: chose

* John Hunt Gent Maior.

[1674]

12th Aprill Vicechancelors wife dyed
Sunday morning dyed Mrs Spencer, of the small Pox shee being the wife of Dr Spencer Master of Bennet Colledge in Cambridge who was then Vice Chancelor of the said Vniuersity; *shee was buryed the same night in St Bennets Church.*

14th Apr Dr Beaumonts daughter dyed
Tewsday morning dyed Beaumont daughter of Dr Beaumont Master of Peterhouse of the small pox at the said Colledge; *she was about 16 yeares old when shee dyed.*

25 Apr Mr Barton found dead
Saturday morning St Markes day Mr Francis Barton one of the senior Fellowes of Trinity Colledge in Cambridge was found dead at the bottome of his Stayres in the house in St Edwards Parish where he dwelt, it being conceived that he fell downe, and had soe laine dead a day or two before it was found out.

26th Apr Mr Copinger dyed
Mr Thomas Copinger minister of Trumpington dyed.

27 Apr Mr Scott Sworne Senior Fellow
Munday Mr Scott sworne Senior Fellow of Trinity Colledge in Cambridge, in the roome of Mr Barton deceased.

4th May Amey
Munday my maydservant Amey came hither to dwell.

14th July Duke of Monmouth chose Chancelor of the Vniuersity of Cambr
Tewsday in the morning at a Congregation in the Regent House in the Vniuersity, was chose his Grace James Duke of Monmouth (the Kings naturall sonne) Chancelour of the Vniuersity of Cambridge in the roome and place of George Duke of Buckingham whose said Place was by Letters from his Majestie signifyed to the Vniuersity to be void, and who recomended the said Duke of Monmouth to the Uniuersity, to succeed in the said Place.

24th Aug Mr Baron Towne Clerke
Bartholomew Common Day Alderman Edward Law resigned upp his Towne Clerkes place, The same Common day was chosen into the same office and place of Towne Clarke Mr William Baron with this provisoe, that he did execute it himselfe onely in case of sicknes or other urgent

---

* Mr John Hunt Major.

occasion to be allowed of by the Maior and the said Mʳ Baron was the same day sworne into the said office, and tooke the other oathes required by Acts of Parliament.

Munday night betweene   dyed Alderman John Herring of a vyolent Fitt of the Stone which held him for about 14 dayes together, in all which time he vomited much, being much afflicted alsoe with the Gout; 21ᵗʰ Sept Alderman Herring dyed

the Bell rang not for him till the next morning about 6 of the Clock. Hee was buryed in Gᵗ Sᵗ Maryes *middle* Chancell about the middle of it, on Thirsday in the afternoone betweene 5 and 6 of the Clock *being the* 24 *Sept* 1674 Mʳˢ (sic) Gibbs that parish minister preached his Funerall Sermon out of Samuel upon these words of King David upon the death of his childe : I shall goe to it but yt shall not retourne to mee. was buryed the 24 Sept

Tewsday in the afternoone betweene 4 and 5 of the Clock, my sonne John Newton was bound apprentice to Mʳ George Pochin Dry Salter for the terme of 8 yeares from the 25ᵗʰ March last past 1674. 17ᵗʰ November Jo Newton bound apprentice

[1674/5*]

Tewsday after Twelfth day at a Grand Common day William Baron had his patent for Towne Clerke then granted to him and sealed, before it was sealed he read it publiquely in the Hall. It was to this effect That the Mayor Bayliffs and Burgesses constituted and appointed him in the Office of Towne Clerke and did grant to him the same office *as fully as Mʳ Law or any before him had the same.* To hold *exercise execute &c.* the same to him to be executed by him or his sufficient deputy to be allowed by the Maior Bayliffes and Burgesses, And for his Fee he was thereby allowed 5ˡⁱ per annum to be paid quarterly Dated the 12ᵗʰ January 1674 the same day young Samuel Moodey and   Williams came in freemen. 12 Jan Towne Clerke Wᵐ Barons patent sealed

Moody & Williams freemen

* Mʳ James Robson Mayor.

March 15. Mr Nevile Butler dyed	Munday dyed Mr Nevile Butler of Barnewell Abbey.

[1675]

April 7. Alderman Wms dyed	Wednesday morning about 8 of the Clock dyed Alderman Philip Williams of Cambridge.
Aprill 13th Cosin Welbore dyed	Tewsday morning about 8 of the Clock dyed my cosin Philip Welbore Esquire at Foxton.
June 6th Mr Atkinson dyed	Sunday about noone dyed Mr Troylus Atkinson bookseller, the bell of Gt St Maryes began to ring for him about 3 of the Clock after prayers ended.
July 26th Dr Wells Master of Queenes dyed	Tewsday morning dyed Dr Wells the master of Queenes Colledge in Cambridge, he was taken suddenly sick in his studdy on the Saturday before being the 24 July 1675, he was buryed in the Chappell of the said Colledge on Wednesday night the 28th July 1675. This day it is reported that Doctor Belke of that Colledge is to succeed in that Mastershipp.
Mr James admd Mr of Queenes	But on the next morning being Thirsday the 29th July 1675 came downe from London to that Colledge Mr James one of the Fellowes of that Colledge with a Mandamus from the King for him the said Mr James to be Master, and he was that morning accordingly admitted Master of the said Colledge, and sworne by Dr Boldero, Vicechancellor, all done before 11 of the Clock that morning, the King alsoe as it is said *then* gave the said Mr James who was one of his Chaplins, a Prebendayryes place of Windsor.
October 10th Mr Frisby dyed	Mr William Frisby the elder Apothecary dyed being Sunday about 5 or 6 in the afternoone, and was buryed on Wednesday following the 13th October 1675.
Coffee houses putt downe	By Proclamacion of his Majestie dated the 29th December 1675 All Coffee houses were prohibited from selling Coffee &c. from and after the 10th January next 167⅘.

* Mr James Robson Maior.

[1676*]

Tewsday morning the 30th May 1676 dyed Alderman Edward Lawe.

Saturday in the afternoone the 23th Sept 1676 dyed Alderman James Robson.

* Mr Andrew Hart Maior.

[1677†]

Saturday morning between 3 and 4 *Fryday night about 10 of the Clock* dyed Doctor Isaac Barrow Master of Trinity Colledge in Cambridge, he dyed at London.

Dr John North had the Mastershipp of Trinity Colledge given him by the King, *and this day came to the Colledge and was admitted Master.*

Munday in the morning dyed Dr   Stevens, who dyed at his house in Jesus Lane in Cambridge.

Munday early in the morning dyed *at Pembroke Hall* Dr Robert Mapletoft Deane of Ely and Master of Pembroke Hall in Cambridge; and the same morning Mr Nathaniel Coga Senior Fellow of the said Colledge was chosen Master thereof.

Mr William Hinton vintner dyed the 24th Oct. 1677 being Wednesday and buryed in *Great* St Maryes Chancell on Fryday night the 26th October 1677.

Samuel Newton and Edward Story bookseller swore Justices of the Peace for the Vniuersity and Towne of Cambridge on Fryday in the afternoone between 4 and 5 of the Clock *being the* 26 *October* 1677 before Samuel Moody one of the Justices of the same Towne and William Baron Towne Clerke *by virtue of a Dedimus to them and the Recorder in that behalfe directed and made* Alderman Crabb being there alsoe present, the same being done at my *new dwelling* house.

† Mr Robert Muriell Maior.

Nov 29 Mr Nich Scot dyed	Mr Nicholas Scott senior dyed being Thirsday in the afternoone towards night.
Nov 30 Dr North sworne a Justice of pease for the County of Cambridge	Fryday about 6 of the clock at night Dr John North Master of Trinity Colledge was sworne at Dr Theophilus Dillinghams Chamber in Clare Hall a Justice of Pease for the County of Cambridge, by the said Dr Dillingham by virtue of a Comission to him and others directed in the presence of me S. Newton.
Decemb 1st John Dunbar dyed	On Saturday morning about One of the clock dyed John Dunbar at the Whitehart.
Dec 30 Mr Storyes & my receiving the Sacrament as Justices of the Peace	Sunday Mr Edward Story with my selfe received the holy Sacrament at Great St Maryes Church it was given us by Mr Robert Scott Minister of that parish in the presence of Thomas King Churchwarden there, and of John Frohock and William Caiton witnesses to our receiving the same I alsoe did see the said Mr Story receive the Sacrament in both kindes from the hands of Mr Scott, and did alsoe see Mr Scott and Mr King subscribe the Certificate for Mr Story, and the like did Mr Story see as to mee both in the said Minister's giving and my receiving the Sacrament and did alsoe *see* the same Minister and Churchwarden then subscribe my Certificate *and at the Sessions following for this County at the Castle I delivered in my Certificate and tooke the oathes &c.*

[167$\frac{7}{8}$]

20th Febr.	Dr Womack then by Dr Spenser Deane of Ely sworne Sub Deane of Ely in the low roome or little parlor of the said Deane in Bennet Colledge before me S. Newton Notary Public, present then Dr Beaumont Master of Peterhouse and John Cranwell.
20 Febr	John Cranwell then by Dr Spenser predict' sworne Auditor of the Church of Ely aforesaid in the said Parlor before me S. Newton Notary public present alsoe then Dr Beaumont Dr Womack.

* Mr Edw. Miller Maior.

[1678]

At a Common Day then held at the Guildhall in Cambridge I Samuel Newton with *the Maior and* all the Aldermen and Common Counsell then present vizt of the Aldermen, Mʳ Muriell *myselfe* Mʳ Jermin Mʳ Mayfield Mʳ Dickinson, Mʳ Townesend Mʳ Fox, Mʳ Ewin, Mʳ Fowle (who this day came in Alderman in the roome of Alderman Tifford deceased) and myselfe tooke the oath of Alleigance, the Oath of Supremacy, the oath *that* it is not lawfull to take up armes against the King &c. and subscribed the Declaration concerning *the unlawfullnes of* the solemne League and Covenant in pursuance of an Act of Parliament made in the 13ᵗʰ yeare of the Reigne of King Charles the 2ᵈ Intituled An Act for the well governing and regulating Corporacions, of all which there was a parchment roll made to bee a record, to which wee all sett our hands   *Alderman Jermin was this day elected Maior for the yeare to come.*

[margin: 16 Aug. being Fryday Taking the oathes upon the Act for Regulating Corporacions]

Dʳ Theoph. Dillingham Master of Clare Hall dyed on Fryday in the afternoone being the 22ᵗʰ November 1678 His Will beares date the sixteenth day of November 1678 which he then subscribed and sealed in my presence.

[1679]

Mʳ Bryan Kitchingman an old Attorney dyed on Fryday morning being the 26ᵗʰ day of September 1679.

[16$\frac{79}{80}$†]

Thirsday morning was the first day Mʳ Loosemore began to teach my son John to sing to and play upon the base Viall, I am to give him 20ˢ per quarter and hee to come 3 times every weeke, vizᵗ at 9 of the Clock in the morning on Mundayes, Wednesdayes, and Frydayes.

[margin: 12ᵗʰ Febr]

* Mʳ Francis Jermin Major.
† Mʳ Thomas Ewin Maior.

The 26th March 1680 paid Mr Loosemore in full to the 25 March instant 15^s and for the future I have agreed with him to pay him 20^s per quarter for teaching John.

24 Dec. 1680 paid him 30^s in full to this time

and the 29 March 1681 paid him 30^s in full for the Quarter ending last Lady day and 2^s for strings,

paid him the 25 June 1681 in full for the Quarter ending the 24 June instant 30^s.

[1680]

Mr Owen Hamond Draper dyed

On Sunday the 18th day of April 1680 being Low Sunday dyed at Lambeth [Mr Owen Hamond Draper].

St Barnabas day the 11th June A Sturgeon taken in Cambridge betweene the small Bridges and Newnham Mills

Fryday on the backside of Alderman Dickinsons house *in Cambridge next the Causey betweene Small Bridges and Newnham by* or against the Felmongers pitts *there* or thereabouts was taken by a Casting net by Coward a fisherman, a Sturgeon of *very near if not altogether * *full* *near* 2 yards long measured by my Japan Cane I see it measured and it was very near 2 of the lengthes of that Cane which cane with the Ivory head is *aboue* *near* a yard long, The waters were then pretty high about the place where the fish was taken about 4 feet deepe, it was thought to bee seene in Newneham Mill pitt if soe, in its returne it was taken as before.

May 26 Mr Chapman marryed

Wednesday Mr Edward Chapman draper marryed at London to Mr Robert Flacks daughter.

June 30th Mrs Crabb dyed

On Wednesday in the afternoone dyed M^{rs}   Crabb the wife of Alderman Nathaniel Crab and buryed in Great St Maryes Church about the *middle in the South Isle* on Fryday following being the 2^d July 1680, Mr Johnson of Sidney College preached her funerall Sermon on these words of the 1st of Job 'The Lord giveth and the Lord taketh and blessed be the name of the Lord.'

On Munday morning about 5 of the Clock dyed Mrs Day wife of Mr Thomas Day Apothecary

July 5th Mrs Day dyed

Tewsday *about 10* in the morning according to notice overnight from Mr Mayor, This morning betweene 8 and 9 the Maior, Mr Fox New Elect, Sir Robert Wright Deputy Recorder and all the Aldermen in their Scarlet with the Common Councell and other Gownemen in their Habitts went in our Orders to New England where about 10 of the Clock wee mett and saluted with our respects the Dutchesse of Yorke in her Coach with 6 Brownish horses and postilion, in her Coach (which was the third Coach) was the Dutchesse of Yorke herselfe, at the head end on the Right hand, next to her at the same end sat the Lady Anne daughter of the Duke of Yorke at the other end sat the Lady Bellus and the Lady Rosse Common her title from her husband being Irish, but shee an English woman, wee being before New England House on the same side of the way with the House and all in our single ranke, Sir Robert Wright our Deputy Recorder went with the Maior and Aldermen to her Highnes Coach side and made a short speech to her, in which *among other things* he said that neither for buildings nor language we did *not* compare with the University from whence we doubted not shee would in that respect receive ample satisfaccion, but in our respects to her and loyalty to his Majestie wee hoped wee were not behinde any &c. or to that purpose, the Dutchesse hansomely presented her selfe to us by a little as it were inclining her gesture towards us, Mr Recorders speach was short which being ended shee thanked us for our kindnes *in courteous manner* and spoke to the Coachman and bid him GOE ON and soe passed on the Coaches which were in number I think foure or five 2 before and 1 or 2 behinde, Then wee went all Mayor *New Elect Recorder* Aldermen Common Councell and Gownemen to the Towne Hall where wee tarryed an houre or more and had a glasse of wine for all the whole company with rolls cheese and

28 Sept. The dutchesse of Yorke being Dutchesse of Modena and the Lady Anne daughter to the Duke their recepcion

* Mr Thos Ewin Mayor.

beere and then after wee all had dranke, the Gownemen except the *Maior Recorder and* Aldermen all went home and after wee had notice Mr Maior *Mr New Elect in Scarlet* Mr Deputy Recorder *in his Gowne* and the Aldermen in their Scarlet *without any others* went to Sir Thomas Pages house then Provost of Kings Colledge where wee were received by Mr Gorring one of the Seniors and I think then Vice Provost there, and the Maior's mace (that noe offence might be taken) being by the Maior ordered not to be carryed before him, after we came into the Provosts Lodgeings we goeing in at the Back dore against St Edwards Chuine [i.e. Church] Lane wee came at last into the further low Roome next the Garden where the Dutches of Yorke *and severall more Ladyes and others being there* where shee standing on the side next the Garden (not sitting) wee all kist her Highnessesse hand, and *then* taking our leave of her, in the next roome to it wee all *or most* of us alsoe kist the hand of the Lady Anne the Dukes of Yorkes daughter who alsoe stood neere a table there about the middle of the roome, and after wee had thus saluted her shee immediately in our presence went into the other roome where the Dutchesse was and soe wee came away, and in the yard Sir Thomas Page the Provost was there to salute us and soe wee went out at the said Back dore as (I understand) the rest of the Doctors if not come in went out that way and then every of us went to his owne home. The Dutchesse is a very hansome gracious lookt person pretty tall, not very bigg, black eyed, something pale faced and a little outlandish like swarthy couller. The Lady Anne pretty round faced about 14 yeares of age. The mayor or the Towne Clerk gave the Dutchessesse *her* 6 or 8 Lackeyes 2 guynyes, and to *her* 3 Coachmen 10^s to drinke.

14th October Mr Artereall to learn my son French

Thirsday in the afternoone agreed with Mr Michael Artereall Frenchman to teach my son John Newton the French Language, he to come hither for that purpose 3 times every weeke, from 5 to 6 in the afternoone to morrow being Fryday to be the first day and I to give 5^s per month.

17 *Nov.* 1680 Pᵈ 5ˢ. 22 *Dec.* 1680 Pᵈ 5ˢ. 20 *Jan.* 80 Pᵈ 5ˢ. 2 *Marc.* 80 Pᵈ 5ˢ. 6 *Apr.*† 81 Pᵈ 5ˢ. 10 *May* 81 Pᵈ 5ˢ. 2 *June* 81 Pᵈ 5ˢ. *July* 81 Pᵈ 5ˢ. 4 *Aug.* 81 Pᵈ 5ˢ.

Fryday night or Saturday morning early dyed Mʳ John Buck Esquire Beadle at his son Thomas Buck's house at Westwick, and buryed I think on Saturday night the 23th October 1680. *[margin: Octob. 22 Mʳ Joe Buck dyed]*

Munday morning betweene 9 and 11 was chosen Mʳ Martin to be Beadle of this Vniversity, in the roome of the said John Buck. One Mʳ Nurse of Trinity Colledge stood against him, Mʳ Nurse had betweene 50 and 60 votes and Mʳ Martin had about 7 score votes. *[margin: Octob. 25ᵗʰ]*

Sᵗ Symon and Sᵗ Jude, Thirsday Agreed then at the Rose, with Mʳ Thamar Organ maker in the presence of Mʳ George Loosemore Organist for an Organ of 3 stopps vizt A dyapazon, a Flute and a Fifteenth to be delivered me and sett upp at my house tomorrow, For which I then agreed with him to pay him Eleaven Poundes, of which I then gave him in parts one shilling. *[margin: Oct. 28. Agreed for my organ]*

On this Sunday night being frost and snow and a cleere starlight night, about 6 of the Clock I saw at the feild back gate of Kings Colledge the streame of the Comett which arose as it were out of a Cloud or thick Sky almost full west as it were *from or* over the Hill whereon Barton Winde Mill formerly stood, at the bottome of it, it seemed about halfe a yard in widenes and soe in a streame or ray pointed upp into the *very* firmament east or north east for many poles length soe many as I could not estimate it, *but very long it was* the streame when I saw it was not very bright, but white or somewhat enclineing to yellow, of a great bignes; there was noe star or commett in the Cloud as I could *then* see *or tooke notice of* but the streame arose in such a breadth as before out of the cloud *but on* *[margin: 12ᵗʰ December Commett]*

---

* Mʳ Thomas Fox Maior.

† Both in this list of payments and in the body of the Diary, a new and very black ink begins to be used about this date.

C. A. S. *Octavo Series.* XXIII.

other nights (for it continued many nights) growing lesse and lesse, the starr was plainly seene, which was noe bigger then an ordinary starr but more dull.

21ˢᵗ December
Edᵐ Halfhead marryed

St Thomas Day Tewsday after Sermon in the morning at Great St Maryes Church in Cambridge were marryed Edmund Halfeheid Apothecary and Frances Clerke.

[1681]

8th Aug. Provost of Kings dyed

Munday dyed Sir Thomas Page Provost of Kings Colledge in Cambridge and buryed the 11th August 1681.

7th Aug. Sister Scott & Ald'. Hart dyed

Sunday night about 6 of the Clock dyed my sister Anne Scott, the same night also dyed Alderman Andrew Hart.

10 Aug.

Dr Fairbrother of Kings Colledge dyed.

11th Aug Cosin Edm. Clarke dyed

Thirsday morning about 6 of the Clock dyed my Cosin Edmund Clarke.

[168$\frac{1}{2}$*]

Valentine Day the 14 Feb Mrs Pyke dyed

Tewsday in the forenoone betweene   and   of the clock dyed Mrs Amey Pyke wife of Mr Richard Pyke the Attorney, shee fell sick the Thirsday night next before the day shee dyed her husband was then at London.

[1682]

The 1ˢᵗ of April Morrocco Embassador interteyned at Cambridge

Saturday betweene 11 and 12 in the morning came his Excelency   the Morrocco Embassadour to Cambridge and 3 others of the same Nacion with him in the Kings Coach, and about 6 more of his attendants on horseback, the Embassadour and those in the Coach all alike clad, with kinde of plads or loose garments or Mantles over them the Embassadours was cloath of gold or tissue, the others in the Coach scarlet or red lyned with white, the

* Mr Richard Church Maior 1681

Embassadour had on his head a Capp lyke a night capp close to his head but read silke with some yellow sarsenet lyning that appeared, those on horseback had all or most white mantles or plads and their heads bound with the same, all proper lusty men of a very swarthy Complexion. They were invited hither by the Uniuersity and received onely by them at the Regent Walke, The Maior and Aldermen not appearing; the Vicechancellor and heads in their scarlet and they gave them a banquet in the Regent house, (were?) they had alsoe soused eeles, sturgeon samon of *all* *some of* which the Embassadour and the rest of them eat freely, the Embassadour after the banquet and walking to Trinity Colledge and St Johns being a little indisposed laid downe at the Provosts of Kings Lodgeings and about 5 or 6 of the Clock at the Regent Walke tooke Coach and Horse and departed to Newmarket from whence they came that day. It was not thought fitt by the Maior to complement the Embassadour, it being not usuall for that body to appeare, but to persons of greater quality.

Thirsday towards night dyed Sir Thomas Hatton of Longstanton Baronet. *April 13th Sir Tho Hatton dyed*

Saturday night just at 12 a clock dyed Mrs Sarah Simpson widdow and buryed in her husbands grave in Great St Maryes middle Chancell at the upper end thereof next the north wall on Wednesday in the afternoone being the 7th of June 1682 about 6 of the Clock, Mr Scott of Sidney Colledge preached her funerall Sermon on these words in the 26 Acts and 8 verse Why should it be thought a thing incredible with you, That God should rayse the dead? *June 3^d Mrs Simpson widdow dyed*

Saturday night about 8 of the Clock dyed Dr Gilbert Wigmore and was carryed to Shelford to be buryed. *Aug 12th Dr Gilbert Wigmore dyed*

Saturday about halfe an houre after 3 in the afternoone dyed Mr Robert Muriell Alderman of Cambridge and Captaine of the Trained Band there. *Sept. 2^d Ald: Muriell dyed*

* Mr Richard Church Major.

[1682/3]

22th March
Fire at Newmarket

Thursday about 9 of the clock that night began a great fire at Newmarket his Majestie King Charles the 2ᵈ being then there at his owne house with the Queene Catherine his Consort and his Royall brother James Duke of Yorke which fire began in a Reeke of straw or hame as was said by the carelesnes of some person having a torch in his hand, it began on Suffolke side within 2 or 3 houses of the little stone bridge neare the market place and burnt downe all that side of the street with the market place and out houses from where it began to the further end of the Towne towards Bury excepting 2 or 3 houses, the winde being very high and a South winde onely that *part of the* side was burnt, but the other side being in danger it was resolved that his Majestie and Court should that night come to Cambridge and accordingly word came to the Vice Chancellor about one of the clock on Fryday morning, who immediately gave order for Great Sᵗ Maryes Bells to Jangle to give notice to the Towne and Candles &c. to be in all places alight, and accordingly the Bells did jangle and Candles in abundance in all parts of the publick streetes on both sides in their windows lighted, and the King and Court accordingly expected. But betweene 2 or 3 in that morning there came the Lord *Grandison* to the Dolphin and acquainted Mʳ Maior, that his Majestie would goe or was gone to Cheavely and not come to Cambridge but his Majestie did not stirr from Newmarket but continued there all night, and went away from thence not till Munday following being the 26ᵗʰ March 1683.

[1683]

26ᵗʰ March
Mʳ Richardson Beadle dead

Munday morning Purbeck Richardson one of the Esquire Beadles of the University of Cambridge *betweene 8 and 9 of the Clock shott himselfe with a birding peice, he did it* wilfully but the Jury of the Coroner found upon their enquiry he was not compos mentis.

     following was John Perne of Peterhouse chosen Beadle in the roome of Richardson.   *Mr Perne chosen Beadle*

 Fryday morning about *Five* of the clocke dyed the Honorable and the Reverend John North Doctor in Divinity and Master of Trinity College in Cambridge.   *13 Aprill Dr North Master of Tr. Coll dyed.*

 Munday night at 8 of the Clock dyed Mr Clement Nevill the *most* Senior Fellow of Trinity Colledge in Cambridge aged in February last 80 yeares *he was buryed in Castle Camps chancell on Saturday following the 5th May* 1683.   *30th April Clem^t Nevill Esqr dyed*

 Wednesday *Thirsday* came Dr John Mountague (Master of Trinity Colledge in Cambridge) to the Colledge being the first time he came as Master. The Vice Master and most of the Fellowes with seuerall others rode out to to meet him, and from thence conducted him to the Colledge.   *3^d May Dr Mountague came Master to Tr. Coll*

 Mr Richard Ray Butler of the Lower Butteryes in Trinity Colledge in Cambridge dyed this morning (as it was said) about 4 of the Clock of the small pox.   *2^d May Mr Rich. Ray dyed*

 Mr Richard Church Major 1681 [*sic*].

 Roger Hurst Carryer by an Elegit seized on Mr Richard Church the Mayor his wine and goodes as it was said for 700^{li} he was bound for.   *Fryday*

 Robert Muriel admitted Butler of the Upper Butteryes in Trinity Colledge he paying yearely to his mother for her life 20^{li} per annum and to his brother Charles for his life 12^{li} per annum.

 Robert Martin admitted Butler of the Lower Butteryes in Trinity Colledge he paying yearely to Mrs Ray widdow towards the maintenance of her and her children 20^{li} per annum as long as shee continues a widdow and after for the better maintenance of her children as the Master and Seniors shall thinke fitt.

 Sunday in the   dyed the Reverend learned and worthy Dr Benjamin Whitchcott, at Dr Cudworths Lodgeings at Christs Colledge in Cambridge.   *13th May Dr Whitchcott dyed.*

July 4th
Mr Sparkes
dyed

Wednesday in the afternoone about   of the clock dyed Mr John Sparkes the elder baker.

Wm Pedder on Munday night about 9 of the Clock being the 30th July 1683 dyed of the small pox, being the 6th day of his sicknes.

Alderman John Ilger on Thursday morning early being the 21th September 1683 was found dead in his bedd he was laid into his grave in St Edwards Church that night his funerall was on Fryday night the 21 September 1683.

Alderman Richard Church (being then Maior) on Fryday dyed being the 28th Sept. 1683 being the 2nd yeare of his Majoralty.

Mr Nathaniel Crabb Maior.

Samuell Newton Junr chose Alderman.

On Tewsday the 23rd October 1683 [Samuel Newton jun.] chose Alderman of Cambridge in the roome of Mr Richard Church deceased and sworne on Fryday following at a Common Day then held being the 26th October 1683.

Samll Newton Junr married his 2d wife

On Munday the 29th October 1683 [Sam. Newton jun.] married Elizabeth Rogers his Second wife at Exning by Mr Peachey Minister there.

[168¾*]

Mr Hugh Martin & Mrs Mary Simpson married 5th Febr.

Hugh Martin one of the Esquire Beadles of the University of Cambridge and Mrs Mary Simpson were married in Emanuel Colledge Chappell by Dr   Bolderston Master of that Colledge, on Tewsday morning *being the 5th February* 1683 betweene the houres of 9 and 10, Dr Nathanael Coga Master of Pembroke Hall gave them in marriage present then onely Dr Bolderston and his wife, Dr Coga and mee Samuel Newton, it was *a* fine sunshine morning the great frost which had continued above 2 months breaking or thawing that morning.

GREAT FROST.

Memorandum that a frost began about 28th November 1683 and continued untill Tewsday the 5th February 1683

* Mr Nathanael Crabb Maior.

(there being in that time onely about 4 or 5 dayes of Thaugh) In which Frost the Thames at London *were* *was* frozen on which there were then many boothes and shopps for many dayes together; a horse race was run on the Ice, a Bull bated thereon: The Sea at Deale was frozen 2 miles from the Shore, and on the coast of Holland particularly off of Sceveling the Sea was frozen 8 leagues from shore and that in 16 fathom water they had mett with ice strong enough to beare, some haveing bin on it; On the said 5th February 1683 (being New moon that day 17 minutes before noone) it began to Thaw *and continued so as that the frost quite broke.*

[1684]

Fryday betweene 6 and 7 of the clock in the afternoone, in the forechamber of Alderman Thomas Fowle was hee the said Thomas Fowle sworne Justice of the Peace of the Towne and University of Cambridge by Dr Edward Stoyte, mee Samuel Newton and William Baron by virtue of his Majesties Writt or dedimus to us directed bearing date the 1st March 1683 in the 36th year of his Majesties Reigne. *April 11th.*

Mr Nicholas Eagle Maior 1684.

[168⅘]

Sunday morning about 4 a clock dyed William Lord Allington at his House in Horseheath *and buryed at Horseheath on Tewsday night the 17th Feb. 1684.* *Febr. 1st Ld Allington dyed*

On Munday morning about 8 of the Clock our Soueraigne Lord King Charles the Second, was taken with a vyolent fitt, which held him above an houre, but by being let bloud through Gods mercye he did revive and great hopes there is of his recovery God be praysed. *Febr. 2^d King Charles the 2^d fell sick*

Saturday it is this day about 10 of the clock *it was* or betweene 10 and 11 this morning *it was* commonly re- *Febr. 7. Kg Charles the 2^d dyed* ported in Cambridge (*and which proved true*) that *the* King Charles the 2ᵈ *was* *is* dead and that he dyed *yesterday about 10 or 11 of the clock in the morning* *this last night* *being Fryday the 6ᵗʰ February* 1684 and that his brother his Royall highnes *the* *James* Duke of Yorke was in London about 4 *or* 5 of the clock *this morning* *yesterday in the afternoone being Fryday 6ᵗʰ February* 1684 proclaimed King, whome God long preserve.

9ᵗʰ Febr.
Kᵍ James the 2ᵈ proclaimed

On *Munday* His Majestie King James the 2ᵈ was *in Cambridge* proclaimed King of England Scotland France and Ireland, by the Maior Aldermen Common Counsellmen Bayliffes and other Freemen *of Cambridge* on horseback all Gownemen in their Gownes, the Maior and Aldermen in Scarlett, about ten of the clock in the morning, before any Order came to them from London, His Majestie was proclaimed *by them* in 8 places of the Towne 1ˢᵗ at the great market Crosse, 2 on the same Market place betweene the Conduit and the Rose Taverne, 3 at Jesus Lane end against the Dolphin, 4 just on this side the Great Bridge, 5 against Sᵗ Giles Church beyound the Great Bridge, 6 against Trinity College, 7 against Buttolphs Church 8ˡʸ and lastly on the Peasemarket Hill; In all those places I Samuel Newton by the request of Mʳ Eagle Maior read the Proclamacion and Mʳ Baron Towne Clerke pronounced the same after mee with an audible voyce.

14 Feb.
King Charles the 2ᵈ interred

Saturday in the Evening was his late Majesty King Charles the 2ᵈ interred in the Chappell of King Henry the 7ᵗʰ at Westminster Abbey, in a very hansome and decent order as could bee for a private Funerall.

A Coppy of the Towne of Cambridge their Addresse to His Majestie King James the 2ᵈ.

To the Kings most Excellent Majestie
Wee the Mayor Bayliffes and Burgesses of your Majesties Towne of Cambridge doe most sincerely blesse Almighty God for your Majesties just and happy establishment in the Throne of your Royall Ancestors.

All our lives and Fortunes are your Sacred Majesties And shall dayly be employed to preserve your Majestie in your Royall Seat.

And that the Succession of the Imperiall Crowne of these your Majesties Realmes may for ever continue in your Royall Line.

Lett all your People (with the same minde and resolucion as wee doe) say

Amen.

Given under the Common Seale of our Towne with free and unanimous consent the 24th day of February in the First year of your Majesties Reigne.

[1685]

Mrs *Elizabeth* Story Captain Storys wife Mr Crabbs sister dyed on this 12th August 1685 being Wednesday in the morning.

<small>12th Aug Mrs Story dyed</small>

[168⅚]

being Wednesday in the morning dyed Mr Owen Mayfield Alderman of Cambridge.

<small>27th Jan. Alderman Owen Mayfield dyed</small>

[1686]

Mrs Elizabeth Sparkes Widdow sickned on Wednesday night the 12th May, dyed on the Tewsday following between 6 and 7 in the afternoone being the 18th May of a violent feaver and buryed in St Edwards Churchyard next her husband on Thursday following in the afternoone between 6 and 7 of the Clock being the 20th May 1686.

<small>Mrs Sparkes dyed</small>

Thursday the 14th October 1686 being the birthday of his Majestie King James the 2^d John Bever Baker was marryed to Susanna Bowes alias Bowles, in Emanuel College Chappel by Mr Iliffe Fellow of that College.

<small>John Bever & Susanna Bowes marryed</small>

[168¾]

4th Jan*y*
Mr Basset
Master of
Sidney
Dr Minshall
deceased.

    being Tewsday Mr Basset Fellow of Caius College had his Majesties Mandate to be Master of Sidney Sussex College, which this *night* *Tewsday morning about 9 of the Clock* was brought downe to Cambridge and delivered at Sidney College; *requiring them to elect and chuse the said Mr Basset to be their Master, the Mastershipp being then voyd by the death of Dr Minshall late Master who dyed on Fryday night the 31th December last 1686 his funerall was on Munday in the afternoone being the 10th January 1686* one whome they called Father Francis of the Romish Church delivered it to the College and Mr Bolt and Mr Holman University Register being 2 Fellows of Caius College went with Father Francis to Sidney College ... [when?] he delivered it.

6th January
Mr Geo Griffith Schoolemr dyed

    being *Fryday in the morning* *Thursday about 6' of the clock in the afternoone* dyed Mr George Griffith Schoolemaster of the Freeschoole in Cambridge *hee was laid in the ground in St Edwards Chancel on Sunday night following betweene 8 and 9 of the clock, his funerall was on Tewsday in the afternoone being the 11th day of January 1686.*

9th Jan*y*
Mr Edward Sparkes Schoolemaster

    being Sunday after Evening Chappell at Caius College was Mr Edward Sparkes admitted Master of Dr Perses Free Schoole in Cambridge, in the roome of Mr Griffith deceased.

26th February Sarah Newton dyed.

    My cosin Sarah Newton daughter of my nephew Samuel Newton and of Sarah his late deceased wife dyed on this morning being Saturday about 6 of the clock or about a quarter of an hower after 6 *and shee was buryed on Tewsday following in the afternoone betweene 5 and 6 of the clock being the first day of March 1686 in the Churchyard of St Bennet in Cambridge in the same grave wherein my brother John Newton was buryed.*

* Mr Isaac Watlington Maior.

[1687]

Sunday morning dyed Mr Martin Buck Apothecary about 2 in the morning and buryed on Tewsday the 9th August 1687 about 6 in the afternoone at the upper end of the South Isle of St Edwards parish Church next unto his wife.

7th August Mr Martin Buck dyed

Saturday morning about 4 of the clock dyed Dr Lewis at his Chamber in Jesus College in Cambridge.

13 Aug Dr Lewis dyed

Sunday morning *Saturday Evening* about   of the clock dyed Mr Edward Wilson late one of the Aldermen of the Towne of Cambridge.

*Aug. *14* 13. Mr Edw. Wilson dyed*

Thursday about 5 of the clock this morning dyed the Reverend and learned D^r   More, Doctor in Divinity Fellow of Christs College in Cambridge, at his chamber there *and buryed in Christs College Chappell the Saturday following.*

1st September Dr More dyed

Sunday Sarah Nicholson daughter of Robert Nicholson of Cambridge stationer married at Trinity College Chappell by *Dr Wolfran Stubb* unto Robert Dawney of the Citty of Norwich worsted weaver son of Anne Keeling of Norwich widdow.

11th Septr Sarah Nicholson marryed to Robert Dawney

Fryday in the Evening about 6 of the clock Alderman Mathew Blackley came to mee to my dwellinghouse and desired mee to goe along with him to Mr Isaac Watlington then Maior of Cambridge and shewed mee a Letter sealed with His Majesties Seale Manuel directed to the Maior and Aldermen of Cambridge and all others whome it may concerne the contents whereof I knew not I did not aske him what it concern'd, neither did he then tell me, I tould him I would wait upon him to the Maior, soe he went and fetcht Mr Nathanael Crabb to my house, as I take it from Dr Stoyts where hee had as I believe left him, and soe wee all 3 went to Mr Mayors, who being not within at his house, he was sent for from the Rose where he was, who after a little while came to us, and then Mr Blackley presented the said Letter to Mr Mayor which he presently

16th Septr His Maties Letter concerning Ald. Blackley

opened and read which Letter was Dated at the Court at Bath the 10th September 1687. The contents of which letter was That Whereas His Majestie had received a good carracter of the said Mr Blackley and of his ability to serve as Mayor of the said Corporacion of Cambridge, It was His will and pleasure that he should be chosen into the same office and admitted Mayor of the said Towne for the next ensueing yeare *without takeing any oathes whatsoever excepting the oath usually given for the executing the said office* His Majestie *thereby* dispensing as he did thereby dispense *with the taking* *with* for his taking any oathes excepting the oath for executing the said office, or to this effect, soe Mr Maior tould him he would assoone as conveniently might be call the Aldermen together and comunicate the said Letter to them, which he did the next day being Saturday betweene 2 and 3 of the clock in the afternoone, all of the Aldermen with Mr Fage New Elect then meeting and present except Mr Fowle who was then at the Fayre, but afterwards that Evening came to the Rose to us.

[168$\frac{7}{8}$]

8th March
Mr Walker made Dor in Physick

Mr William Walker Apothecary by the Kings Mandate was at the University Schooles created Doctor in Physick in the afternoone of this day being Thursday the 8th March 1687.

[1688]

26 Apr.

Wednesday at a Common day about 4 in the afternoone, a messinger brought downe two orders from the King and Counsell bearing date the 18th of Aprill 1688, the one for removeing the Mayor 5 Aldermen 12 Common Counsell men and the Towne Clerke, the other for the Electing and admitting of a new Mayor 5 Aldermen, 12 Common Counsell men and a Towne Clerke.

[1688]   ALDERMAN NEWTON'S DIARY.

The names of them that were putt out & removed were these.

The names of those that came new in, in the roome of those that were putt out were these.

Out	New putt in
John Page, Mayor	Nathanael Crabb, Mayor
Samⁿ. Newton, Justice of the Peace & Alderman	Edward Story, Justice & Alderman
Francis Jarmin, Justice of the Peace & Alderman	John Frohock, Alderman
Thomas Ewin, Alderman	Richard Berry, Justice & Alderman
Thomas Fox, Alderman	Peter Lightfoot, Alderman
Thomas Fowle, Alderman	John Townesend, Alderman

Common Councellmen

Thomas Dickinson	John Gilbert
Phillip Hawkins	Daniel Love, Jun.
John Walker	Thomas Lowry
Corn. Austin	Richard Lindsey
John Saunders	John Blackley
Wᵐ. Wendey	James Wendy
Adam Newlin	Peter Settle
Nicholas Apthorpe	John Chaplin
John Disborough	Philip Pearson
Thomas Riches	Richard Pearson
John Dennys	Thomas Wendy
Henry Pyke	Peter Cooke
William Baron, Towne Clerke	Francis Webb, Towne Clerke

Vpon Tewsday at a Common Day being Hock Tewsday the 1ˢᵗ day of May 1688 by Order from the King & Counsell.

New Putt in
Mr Gimbert, Alderman
Mr Skeiring, Alderman
Mr Hawkes, Alderman
Mr Clay, Alderman
Mr Marshall, Alderman
Mr Northrope, Alderman

Common Counsell
Samᵘ Potter
Wᵐ Fuller
Ralph Long

Jo. Lindsey
Artemus Hinde
Tho. Thompson
Tho. Bland
Charles Bumpstead
Symonds
Petkins
Taylor of Chesterton
Ellis

[The next page is left blank.]

8th June
Bishopps comitted to the Tower

On Fryday, the Arch Bishopp of Canterbury with 6 other Bishopps appeared before the King and Counsell, and were the same day committed to the Tower, whither they were conveyed the same day by water in the Arch Bishopps Barge.

9th June
James Ramsey dyed

On Saturday night about 12 of the clock dyed James Ramsey taylor.

10th June
Dr Withrington dyed

On Sunday dyed Dr Withrington Fellow of Christs College in Cambridge who was the Lady Margarets Professor of Divinity.

11th June

Being Munday St Barnaby's day Its said, That there is a Prince of Wales borne, whome God preserve in health and make him a blessing to this Nation.

Prince of Wales borne on Sunday the 10th June 1688

It is this day further confirmed that the Queens Majestie was yesterday the 10th of June 1688 being Sunday delivered of the Prince of Wales about 10 of the clock in the forenoone, this Munday night upon that occasion Great St Maryes Bells rang and a Bonfire was on the Great Hill in Cambridge and the souldiers there mett and gave severall volleys of shott.

16th June
Dr Gowarth Mar of St Johns chose Margarets Professor

being Saturday in the forenoone was chose Dr Gowarth Master of St Johns to bee the Lady Margarets Professor in Divinity, in the roome of Dr Widdrington lately deceased

26th June
Dr Cudworth dyed

being Tewsday about 8 of the clock in the morning dyed Dr Ralph Cudworth Master of Christ College in Cambridge

Hebrew Professor of the Vniversity and Prebendary of Gloucester the distemper was a stoppage of his vrine.

Mrs Worts after a very hard and hazardous labour was this Saturday morning delivered of her son, *which within one month after dyed*   30th June

Saturday by Nathanael Sawyer the Carryer newes was brought that the 7 Bishopps Tryal being yesterday the jury acquitted them for which deliverance God be praised; *but the Juryes verdict for the Bishopps was not given in till this Saturday morning*   30th June Brps acquitted

Mr Hayes the printer said that His Majestie had bestowed the mastershipp of Christs College upon Mr Smithson one of the Fellows of that College, *but it was not soe His Majestie giveing that mastershipp to Dr Colvile.*   30th June New Mar. of Christ Coll.

Wolfran Stubbe Dr in Divinity on Fryday morning was elected Hebrew Professor of the University of Cambridge in the roome of Dr Cudworth lately deceased.   6 July Dr Stubbe Hebrew Professor

On Saturday Doctor Colvile was elected Master of Christs Colledge in Cambridge in the roome of Dr Cudworth lately deceased   7th July Dor Colvile Mar of Xt Coll.

Mr Thomas Peters Vphoulster about one of the clock this morning being Thursday dyed, hee was on Munday night last taken with a vomiting and loosenes and that being prety well of, and somewhat better on Wednesday in the afternoone was upp and walkt in his chamber, but findeing himselfe faint laydowne and afterwards went to bed and being in deadly cold clammy sweats soone after in the night time dyed *and was privately without publick funerall buryed on Fryday night being the 3d August* 1688.   2nd August Mr Tho. Peters dyed

being Munday in the afternoone dyed Mr Thomas Buck son of Mr Thomas Buck of Westwick *and the next night being Tewsday carryed to Okeington and buryed there*   6th August Mr Buck Jun dyed.

being thirsday in the afternoone was chosen Mr Matthew Blackley baker New Elect hee being as is reported a Roman Catholique, the 2 persons that came out of the box were Samuel Potter Cordwainer William Symons miller, The Electors were   Gilbert senr the cooper Artemus Hinde   16th August Mr Blackley New Elect

James Wendy butcher John Blackley, James Blackley, young Love, Lindsey &c.

4ᵗʰ October
Mʳ Roger Peapys dyed.

being Wednesday dyed Mʳ Roger Peapys of Impington late Recorder of Cambridge

22 Oct. according to His Maᵗⁱᵉˢ Proclⁿ, the Mayor Alderm. Common Counsel lately put out now restored

Munday in the afternoone at a Common Day in the Hall summoned by Mʳ Nicholas Eagle Mayor according to his Majesties Proclamacion dated the 19ᵗʰ Oct. instant 1688 The Maior Aldermen, Common Councill, Towne Clerke &c Tooke our places in the Hall and there then according to the Towne Orders being a new Elecion Mʳ John Fage, was elected and sworne Maior upon which Mʳ Eagle gave *upp* his place of Majoralty, and wee all tooke the oath of Alderman, Common Councill Towne Clerke Bayliffs Treasurers Sergeants &c and all tooke the oathes required by Act of Parliament Mʳ Felsted then resigned up his place of Alderman and his fine wholly remitted, Mʳ Watlington and Mʳ Fage tooke againe the oathes of Freeman and past offices and chose into the Common Councill againe in the places then voyd, and after at the same Common day were chose Aldermen Mʳ Watlington in the roome of Mʳ Miller deceased and Mʳ Fage in the roome of Alderman Mayfield deceased, by order then made to have their Seniority and precedency according as they were when removed before by the Kings Order, and Mʳ Peapys was chose Alderman in the roome of Mʳ Felsted.

7ᵗʰ November

Wednesday. This day newes came in the publick Letters to this Towne, That the Dutch were landed on Munday last at Dartmouth in Devonsheire.

13ᵗʰ December

This night and severall nights before there were upp in armes a great many in this Towne *some nights* 2 or 300 (*many scholars among them*) of the rabble called the Mobile who at first under a pretence to seeke for papists and such who had favoured them and to ransack their houses for armes, at last came to be very insulting and wherever they pleased to enter mens houses and doe them much mischeife.

14ᵗʰ December

Fryday at night betweene 8 and 9 of the clock at night it was reported by one Turkinton that came from or about

---

* Mʳ Fage Maior.

Huntington that 5 or 6000 of the Irish lately disbanded had burnt Bedford and cutt all their throats there and they were comeing on for Cambridge to doe the like there, whereupon all this whole Towne was in an uproare and fearfull crying out all about the Towne and all presently upp in armes *crying out in the streets arme arme for the Lords sake,* and it being a rayny and darke night candles *alight* were sett upp in all windowes next the streetes, and it was said that they were comeing in at the Castle end, others said they were come in and cutting of throats, soe that the scare for the present was very great and dismall many running and rideing out of Towne to escape the danger, till it was considered how improbable such a thing should bee soe of a sudden, and besides wee *are* were informed from some who came that afternoone from Bedford and that way and they neither see any Irish nor heard of any such comeing in to those parts or this way, and so the Towne about 10 of the clock that Evening or before began to bee free from any such feares. *The Irish reported to be a comeing to Cambridge in a hostile manner*

sometime this last weeke his Majestie King James the second being at Rochester at Sir   Heads house, privately went away from thence and passed over in *to* France as it is generally reported. *31 Dec. King James passed over Sea into France*

[168⅞]

Fryday morning at a Common day by adjornement from a generall Common day holden the Tewsday next before being the 8th January instant 1688 was chosen Sir Thomas Chicheley Knight and John Cotton Esquire for persons to meet at Westminster at the Convention on the 22th instant January; I was not at the Eleccion. *11 Janry*

Tewsday at the Castle was elected to meet at the said Convencion Sir Levinus Bennet and Sir Robert Cotton for the County of Cambridge I was not at this Eleccion *15 Janry*

and on the same Tewsday *in the afternoone* was elected *15 Janry* for the University of Cambridge to meet at the said Convencion Sir Robert Sawyer Knight and Mʳ Isaac Newton Mathematique Professor of the University of Cambridge and Fellow of Trinity College in Cambridge.

21ᵗʰ Jan⁷ Doʳ Green marryed Mʳˢ Susanna Flack Munday marryed at Linton Greene Doctor in Physick and Mʳˢ Susanna Flack

22 Jan⁷ Tewsday mett the Convencion at Westminster

1ˢᵗ Febr Fryday in the afternoone at Bennet Church was by Mʳ Kidman Minister there, baptized Samuel Newton son of my nephew Samuel Newton, Mʳ Arthur Rogers and I were godfathers and Mʳˢ Everard and Mʳˢ Halfhyde godmothers. hee was borne on   being the   of January 1688.

8ᵗʰ Febr. Fryday in the publick Letter at the Coffee house it was reported that yesterday or day before it was voted in the Convension, as well by the Major part of the Lords house as House of Commons that the Prince and Princes of Orrange should be crowned King and Queene of England, yet that nevertheles 37 of the house of Lords whereof was 12 Bishopps there votes was against *it* but the major part of that house which were 55 carryed *it*, the said 12 Bishopps then protesting against it.

14 Febr. Thirsday this day by Order from the Lords spirituall and temporall in the Convension assembled was kept as *a* day of publique thanksgiving (to God Almighty) in Cambridge and els where in the severall Countyes for Gods gracious deliverance of us from Popery and arbetrary governement and Mʳ Laughton of Trinity College preached at Sᵗ Maryes his text in the   psalme and the last verse and this day alsoe printed proclamacions came downe to Cambridge of the forme of proclayming of *William* Henry Prince of Orange and Mary Princesse of Orange King and Queene of England France and Irelande and the Territoryes thereunto belonging and it was said (*and is true*) they were proclaymed at London yesterday King and Queene according to the

* Mʳ Fago Maior.

said proclamacion *this day it was alsoe reported that King James the 2ᵈ was taken in a ship goeing from France to Ireland but that report was false.*

being Munday was in the afternoone *betweene 2 and 3 of the clock* of the same day proclaimed by the Mayor Bayliffes and Burgesses of the Towne of Cambridge William Prince of Orange and Mary Princesse of Orange, King and Queene of England France and Ireland and the Territoryes thereto belonging, the Maior and Aldermen in Scarlett on horseback and the Common Counsill on Horseback in their Gownes with many that had past offices and other Freeman, first *they were* proclaimed at the Market Crosse, 2ˡʸ on the market place on the Hill neare the Rose Taverne, 3ˡʸ on this side *next* the Great Bridge, 4ˡʸ against my Cosin Samuel Newtons house next Kings College Lane called Nutt Lane, 5ˡʸ against Sᵗ Buttolphs Church Lastly on the Peasemarket Hill, Mʳ Fage Maior read the Proclamacion being in print and Mʳ Baron Towne Clerke more audibly repeated it after him, There was noe perticuler Order to the Towne for proclayming it, onely there was a Letter came downe *from the Counsill my Lord Hallifax president and severall others* directed to the Sheriffe of the County of Cambridge or if there bee none then to the Coroner or Coroners of the same County Thereby requiring them to cause the printed Proclamacions therein enclosed to be published in all the usuall places with the solemnityes in such cases used there being 2 Proclamacions one of which for the proclayming King William and his Lady Queene Mary and the other was that all Officers Justices and others &c. in Office should continue and execute their offices till further Order. Now this letter came downe by the Post on last Fryday, but it hapned that both the High Sheriffe and Undersheriffe were at London and soe it lay, none knowing although suspecting the Contents thereof, the Undersherife came not into the Countrey till Sunday in the afternoone and came soone to Cambridge and declared both to the Vice Chancellor and Maior the Contents thereof being Munday morning,

Margin: 18ᵗʰ Febr. Towne proclaimed Kˢ Wᵐ & Queene Mary

7—2

the Vice Chancellor on Saturday or Fryday evening hearing there was a Letter as aforesaid directed, haveing a Consult with the heads sent a messinger on purpose either to the Vniversity Chancellor or as I heard to Mʳ Whyn some Secretary above in Court to know what Order they might expect concerning this matter, which this Munday being not retourned they waited his retourne before they thought it fitt to proclaime, but Mʳ Mayor &c. determined it was sufficient he had notice by the Sheriff (although the Shereffe had nothing but the Letter in Comand) to proclaime this Munday *which he accordingly did* soe the Undersheriffe being Mʳ Jeffery he began this Munday in the afternoone about 2 of the clock to proclaime the King and Queene first in the Castle Yard and then at the Market Crosse immediately after which the Maior &c. proclaimed, attended by all the *Millitary* Officers, with their Trumpetts and Kettle drums and about 50 of their souldiers with their drawne swords, alsoe the Towne waytes played before the whole Company from the Towne Hall to the further end of the great market place, when wee had done proclayming, Mʳ Mayor appointed myselfe and Mʳ Jermin to wait on Sir Richard Bassett the head Captain to wish him and the rest of the officers to drinke a glasse of wine at the Hall and accordingly wee did, and they all came to the Hall and wee had there plenty of wine, and the Trumpetts 6 or 8, and Kettle drums and Towne Waytes Mʳ Mayor on the Towne account gave the Trumpetts and Kettle drumers a guinea, Mʳ Perne (as was supposed) came to the Towne Hall from the Vice Chancellor to invite the officers to a treat the next morning, when the University intended to proclaime the King and Queene, some of the Uniuersity as I was informed by Mʳ Ewin being not well pleased that the Towne should proclaime before them, All the afternoone and at night ringing of bells and at night bonfires, *there was alsoe sent 2 or 3 dozen bottles of wine given by the Towne to the Troopers on the Hill that attended the proclaiming.*

* Mʳ Fage Maior. Doʳ. Colvile of Xt Coll. Vice Chancellor.

The Vicechancellors and heads of Colleges and Doctors in Scarlett on Foot being Tewsday morning about 10 of the Clock with the rest of that body *there* in their Habitts, at the Market Crosse and on the Hill against the Rose Taverne proclaimed King William and Queene Mary Prince and Princesse of Orange to bee King and Queene of England France and Ireland &c. The Officers and some *part* of their Troopes then in Towne attended the service, the officers were invited by the Vice Chancellor to dinner, the souldiers &c. had I heere *5* 10 guineas given them to drinke, likewise the Towne waytes played before them. 19 Feb University proclaimed K^g W^m & Q Mary

Mr Charles Morden this day being Tewsday dyed betweene *one and two* of the clock in the afternoone at the Rose Taverne; and was buryed in St Michaels Church in Cambridge on Thursday in the afternoone about 4 of the clock being the 28th February 1688.

Tewsday the Arch Bishopp of Canterbury 1688 *Chancelour Elect for the University of Cambridge* by his Letter this day dated directed to Dr Colvile Master of Christ College and Vice-Chancelour of the said Vniuersity resigned up his said Chancellourshipp, and therein exprest he expected the Uniuersity aforesaid should according *to* their Statutes within 14 days from the date of his said Letter Elect another person to bee their Chancellour.

Fryday morning *Charles* Duke of Somersett was elected Chancellour of the Uniuersity of Cambridge in the roome of the Arch Bishopp of Canterbury.

[1689]

Fryday night dyed Samuel Newton son of my nephew Samuel Newton and buryed Sunday in the afternoone the 7th April 1689 being then about 11 weekes old.

Monday morning dyed Sir Robert Wright late Lord Cheife Justice of England.

25 June	By vertue of a Dedimus to mee, Mr William Baron and Mr Richard Pyke conjunctim et divisim directed, Mr John Fage Maior, as Mayor was before mee and Mr Baron, sworne a Justice of Peace for the Towne of Cambridge, and hee did then before us alsoe (after he had first taken the oath of a Justice of Peace) take 2 other oathes annexed to the said Dedimus vizt the oath of fidelity and alleigance to King William and Queene Mary, and alsoe another oath to abjure the Pope's authority &c.
4th July	On Thursday morning I S. N. was sworne Justice of the Peace for the Towne of Cambridge by Mr William Baron and Mr Richard Pyke by vertue of the Dedimus above written, and then tooke the oathes above said.
11th July	On Thursday in the afternoone at the Rose Taverne John Pepis one of the Aldermen of the Towne of Cambridge was then sworne Justice of the Peace for the Towne of Cambridge by vertue of the Dedimus above written by Mr William Baron and my selfe.
24th Aug. Provost of K^{gs} Coll dyed	Saturday morning before 4 of the clock being Bartholomews day dyed Dr Coppleston Provost of Kings College in Cambridge *and his funerall was on Fryday night about 9 of the clock, and was buryed in Kings College Chappell in Cambridge.*
29 Aug	The weeke after vizt on Thursday before the King and Councell was heard the matter of Kings College about Mr Isaac Newton, why he or any other not of that Foundacion should be Provost, and after the reasons shewed and argued Mr Newton was laid aside.
2^d Sept	Mr Hartcliffe Fellow of Kings College brought down the Kings Letters to the College to recommend him to be elected their Provost.
3^d Sept^r	being Tewsday and the 10th day from the decease of the old Provost, the College in the morning after service Sermon on that occasion and Sacrament the Fellows went to Eleccion, and notwithstanding the Kings Letter for Mr Hartcliffe, the College elected for their Provost Dr Rodderick master of Eaton Schoole 33 Fellows present Electors, of which but 3 were for Mr Hartcliffe, soe the said

Dr Rodderick after he was elected went to the Bishopp of Lincolne (Kings College Visitor) to Bugden to be admitted, but he did not then admit him takeing some time to consider of it.

  being   dyed Mr Peter Dent sen^r Apothecary and Bachelour in Physick. *Sept. Peter Dent dyed*

  He was buryed in St Sepulchers Church in Cambridge on Thursday night betweene 9 and 10 of the clock being the 5^t day of September 1689.

  Munday morning Mr Hartcliffe Fellow of Kings College, by the Kings Mandate went out Bachelour in Divinity. *23 Sept. Mr Hartcliffe*

  Tewsday Mr Colbourne at the Dolphin, had his goods seised on for debt by Sir John Turner and went away. *24 Sepr. Colbourne*

  Wednesday William Hinton att the 3 Tuns absented himselfe for debt and his *dore and* house shutt up all that day and his goodes as was said seised on by Mr Bowyer. *25 Sept. Hinton*

  Munday morning about halfe an houre after ten, came his Majestie King William to Cambridge, the Maior and Aldermen in Scarlet on Horseback the 24 on foot on Christ College peice, being alighted and kneeling on pesses or matts received him. Mr John Pepys then Maior went and yeilded his Mace to him which the King retourned and then made a short speech and presented from the Corporacion to His Majestie a bason and Ewer of about the value of 33^li brought downe by John Disbrow Goldsmith from London who was sent up thither to buy a cup of about 50^li value but it could not be had, after the mayor ended his speech the maior and aldermen on horseback and the 24 the juniors first and maior next the Kings Coach went before the King to the Regent walke where wee left them and then on horseback went with Mr Maior to his house where the Maior and Aldermen onely at the Corporacion charge dined. The King dyned in Trinity College Hall and about 3 of the Clock went out of Cambridge to Newmarket from whence that morning he came, there was none of the Kings *7 Oct. K^s W^m come to Cambr.*

  * Mr John Pepys Maior.

Mace bearers nor Kettle drum heere nor above 4 or 25* of the Kings guards, George Prince of Denmarke was with the King at the head end of the Coach, and its said 2 dutch Embassadours at the other end for 4 was in the Kings Coach with himselfe, the King goeing to Kings College chappell a peticion or speach was presented to him from that College on the behalfe of Dr Roderick, the King tould them thereupon, that he accepted of their submission and granted their request, which was that Dr Roderick might be the Provost of Kings College.

12 October
Dr Rodderick provost of KingsColl.

Saturday about 3 in the afternoone Do^r Rodderick came to Kings College and *was* admitted Provost thereof.

16 October
L^d of Bedford Recorder

Wednesday at a Common Day in the morning about 11 of the Clock was the Right Honourable William Earle of Bedford elected and sworne a Free Burgesse of the Corporacion of Cambridge, and afterwards in the same forenoon was he elected and sworne Recorder of the Towne of Cambridge and had then alsoe a Patent sealed to him under the Common Seale for that office during his life, and he then tooke the oath of Alleigance to King William and Queene Mary and the other Oath against the Pope or any forreigne power, at the same Common Day were sworne Sir Rushet Cullen of Isleham and Collonel Cutts that had bin at Buda in the Emperors wars against the Turke Free Burgesses of this Towne, my Lord of Bedford then invited the Deputy Maior (Mr Fox) and the Aldermen to dyne with him that day and accordingly we dyned with him at a splendid enterteinement at the Red Lyon, Mr Pepys then Mayor was out of Towne, My Lord being Lord Leivetenant of this County gave us the liberty of nominating to him the Militia officers for this Towne, To whome wee nominated Mr John Pepys for Captaine Mr Thomas Fox Leivtenant and Mr Alderman Henry Pyke *Ensigne* all which my Lord accepted of.

Militia Towne Officers chose.

* i.e. four or five and twenty.

[1690]

On Wednesday dyed Susanna Mayfield at her brother in Law Mr Hookes at Girton daughter of Alderman Mayfield deceased, but buryed in S Edwards Church in Cambridge on Thursday the 3^d of July 1690. *25 June Mrs Sus. Mayfield dyed*

On Sunday morning dyed M^rs   Bryan, the wife of Mr Jarvis Bryan; and shee was buryed in St Edwards Church on Tewsday the 8th July 1690. *6 July Mrs Bryan dyed*

On Tewsday morning dyed Anne Frohock the daughter of my cosin John Frohock, and buryed on Tewsday in the afternoone in Great St Maryes Church the 15 July 1690. *8th July An Frohock dyed*

Saturday Mr Pepys Maior being absent as Captain with his company being then out of Towne and this day at Hinningham in Essex with his company retourning homewards being our Eleccion day for Maior, Mr Thomas Ewin was then Elected Maior for the year ensueing, I Samuel Newton being then Deputy Maior, the whole Company went home then with Mr New Elect and onely sack and clarret but plenty. *16th August Mr Ewin New Elect*

[1691]

Munday morning dyed Mr Thomas Pyke *Clerk* son of Mr Richard Pyke and buryed in St Edwards South Chancell on Wednesday night the 22 July 1691. *20 July Mr Tho Pyke dyed*

Sunday morning about 4 of the clock dyed John Newton son of my cosin Samuel Newton and buryed on Tewsday the 21 July 1691. *19 July Jo. Newton dyed*

Mr William Eversden of Eversden dyed of an Apoplectick fitt. *29 or 30 July Mr Eversden dyed*

Alderman Isaac Watlington married to Mrs Dorothy Dillingham being his 4th wife, he was married at St Sepulchers Church. *30 July Mr Watlington marryed*

* John Pepys Maior.

[169½]

4th Janʸ
Doʳ Babington dyed

Doʳ Humfrey Babington Vice Master of Trinity College in Cambridge dyed of a Apoplexi he fell into it yesterday about 4 in the afternoone and dyed this morning betweene 9 and 10. He dyned yesterday in Hall.

[1692*]

11th June
Doʳ Brakenbury dyed.

30th June
S. N. bapt. & dyed

Saturday night being Sᵗ Barnabas dyed Doʳ Perse Brakenbury of Sᵗ Johns College.
On Thursday was baptized Samuell Newton son of my Nephew Samuel Newton; he dyed on Saturday betweene 12 and one of the clock in the afternoone being the 10th September 1692.

1ˢᵗ Septʳ

On Thursday was baptized Samuel Newton son of my nephew Samuel Newton.

8 September

William Butler marryed to   Carpenter.

8 September Earthquake

being Thirsday *about 2 or betweene 2 and 3 of the clock in the afternoone* there was an Earthquake in Cambridge *at London Ely and severall other parts* but God being mercifull unto us, it did noe harme, onely shaked severall parts in Cambridge and other places it continued but a minute or two.

21 Nov

Munday in the afternoone about 3 or 4 of the Clock in the roome of Sir Robert Sawyer deceased was at a Convocacion held for the University of Cambridge   Boyle Esq elected a Burgesse of Parliament for the said University, Doʳ Brookbanke of Trinity Hall stood against him but lost it, Charles Duke of Somerset Chancelour of the said University was present and satt in the Regent House and tooke the votes   Doʳ Oxendine Master of Trinity Hall being the Elect Vice Chancellour not sworne into that office haveing bin sick and not well recovered at London.

* Mʳ Henry Pyke Maior.

[169⅔]

Saturday about ⎵ in the afternoone dyed Mrs Greene the wife of Do^r^ Christopher Greene, in his dwelling house in St Andrewes parish in Cambridge, it being on that day 4 yeares that they were married. shee on Munday following the 23th January 1692 was carryed in a Hearse coach from Cambridge to Linton and there buryed next her brother Mr George Flack.

21th Jan^ry^ Do^r^ Greenes wife dyed

Tewsday in the afternoone dyed Captain Edward Story.

31th Jan^ry^ Capt Story dyed

[1693]

Saturday in the afternoone about ⎵ of the clock dyed John Spencer Do^r^ in Divinity Master of Bennet College in Cambridge Deane of Ely and Archdeacon of Sudbury he dyed in Bennet College Lodgeings, *and his funerall was on Tewsday in the afternoone being the 11th July 1693 buryed in that College Chappell.*

27^h^ May Do^r^ Spencer dyed

Thursday ⎵ Gimbert Cooke marryed at Grancester Church to Elizabeth Hawkshaw widdow.

*22 June Gimbert marr^d^*

Munday betweene 9 and 10 of the Clock in the forenoone was marryed in St Edwards Church in Cambridge by our minister *M^r^* Tyndale, Alderman Thomas Fox to Mrs Susanna Stoyt in the time of their marryeing it rained.

14 August Alderm Fox marryed. Mr Tho. Walker Mayor

[169¾]

Fryday Dyed Do^r^ Nathanael Coga Master of Pembroke Hall in Cambridge *and into that Mastershipp in his roome on Saturday the 6th February* 1693 *was elected Mr Thomas Browne Minister of Cherry Orton sometime Fellow of that College, and he came to that College and was admitted Master on Thursday the 8th February* 1693.

12th Jan^ry^ Do^r^ Coga dyed & Mr Tho. Browne chosen Mas^r^.

29 Jan⁷⁷ M͏ʳ Scott dyed	Munday in the afternoone dyed Mʳ Robert Scott one of the Senior Fellowes of Trinity College in Cambridge, at his chamber in the same College.
1ˢᵗ March Mʳ Crompton died	Thursday dyed Mʳ Crompton Fellow of Jesus College in Cambridge.
21 March Mʳˢ Bucks man marryed to her servant	Wednesday at Sᵗ Edwards Church in Cambridge was John *Wybrow* servant to Mʳˢ Buck and Margaret Calfe alsoe Mʳˢ Bucks servant marryed.

[1694*]

2ᵈ December Ald. Fage	Sunday dyed Alderman John Fage Vintner about 3 of the clock this morning of a fitt of an Apoplexy, that took him the day before.
28 Decemb.	Fryday, This dayes publique post Letter, mencioned, that our Queene Mary was alive the last night, but in great danger of death, haveing not onely the small pox but withall a high feavour and Sᵗ Anthonys Fire, that by the Order of the Physitians 12 ounces of bloud had bin taken from her and was blistred, that the Court was in Teares and His Majestie drown'd with sorrow.
28 Decemb	dyed Queene Mary, (King Williams Queene) about one of the clock this fryday morning at Kensington *whose funerall being publique was on Tewsday the 5ᵗʰ day of March 1694 being interred in King Henry the 7ᵗʰᵉ Chappell at Westminster.*

[169⅘]

27 Janry Jo. Fullmer	Sunday dyed John Fullmer.
5ᵗ Febr. Doʳ Brattle dyed	Tewsday morning dyed Doctor Daniel Brattle, one of the Senior Fellowes of Trinity College in Cambridge.

* Mʳ Thomas Fox Maior the 2ᵈ time.

[1695]

Thursday at Emmanuel Chappell was Benjamin Young draper and Elizabeth Watlington marryed. *11th April B. Young mar^d*

Munday morning old Alderman Mr William Bryan Confeccioner dyed. *22th April Alderm. Bryan dyed.*

Dyed Alderman Edward Chapman woollen draper in the morning between and 11 of the Clock being Whitson Tewsday; and carryed on Thursday following to Linton being the 16 May 1695 and buryed there in the Chancell. *14 May Alderm. Chapman dyed*

Thursday night I dreamed, that I being in London, there came along Bishopsgate street almost the whole breadth of the street a great many persons haveing along with them a great many dead corps dyeing (as they said) of the plague in plaine coffins not of a black but of a sad couller and the covers not coped but flatt every corps not being borne on their shoulders, but borne *below* by 2 persons one at the head and the other at the feet who by the cord at each end not above a foot from the ground bore the corps along haveing noe hearscloath but the bare flatt coffin, these corps were borne along close one by another *as many as tooke upp* the full breadth of Bishopsgate and entred into and under to goe through that gate, and abundance of people followed the corpses to goe out through the gate *which was throng'd* and I my selfe being then to goe through that gate made some offer, but findeing by the croud it to be very hott and not easily to be passed and besides haveing a fear uppon mee and sadnas at that dismall sight, I turned downe not that street that leades to Moregate I being then on the other side of the way and soe turned downe *that Lane by the gate* that leades the way by London Wall to Algate and soe my dreame ceased leaving sadnes upon my spiritt, Lord be merciful to that great Citty and this whole Nacion Amen Good Lord. *30 May*

21 Novemb Eliz. Fuller married.	Thursday James Howlett of Histon and my cosin Elizabeth Fuller of Hardwick were married at Histon.

[169$\frac{5}{6}$]

31 Jan'7 S. N. son of my Cosin S. N. buryed	Fryday Samuel Newton about 9 or 10 dayes old, was buryed in the Churchyard of St Bennet.
19 Febr. Mr Wm Ayloffe University Oratour	Wednesday *morning* at a Congregacion, at the Vniversity Schooles, was my Cosin William Ayloffe Fellow of Trinity College in Cambridge chosen the Vniversity Oratour of that Vniversity, hee had it but by 4 votes over, Mr Mosse of Bennet College stood against him. *The votes on my cosin Ayloffs side were 95 and on Mr Mosses 91.*

[1696]

30 June	Andrew Baden (my son in law) kept his first Act in the University Schooles in order to his takeing of his Degree of Doctor in Physick and made his Feast that night in Queenes College Hall.

[1697]

7 July Do^r Eachard dyed	towards the Evening of this day being Wednesday dyed Doctor [John] Eachard Master of Katherine Hall in Cambridge at his Lodgeing in the said College.
12 July	being Munday in the morning Do^r Fisher was chosen by the College, Master of Catherine Hall in Cambridge, to succeed Doctor Eachard lately deceased *and after him Sir William Dawes was chosen Master.*
9 Sept.	being Thirsday about 10 of the clock *at night* dyed Mr Henry Pyke Alderman in Prison in Cambridge Castell.
26 Sept. Margery Musson maryed	Sunday at Little St Maryes, was James Alexander and Margery Musson marryed.

[1698]

Thursday at Moulton in Suffolke was Mʳ marryed to my cosin Susanna Harrison.

Read 28 Aprill Sus. Harrison marryed

Saturday morning betweene 5 and 6 of the Clock my Deare wife fell downe next Mʳˢ Chapmans shopp and broke her left Arme, which was sett that morning by my cosin Harrison.

9ᵗʰ July

[1⁶⁹⁹⁄₇₀₀]

Doctor William Lynnett Vice Master of Trinity College in Cambridge being *Sunday* *Saturday* dyed on this day in the night time, and was buryed in Trinity College Chappel on the northside near to the railes at the upper end thereof on the Thursday following being 25 January 1699.

20ᵗʰ January Doʳ Lynnet dyed

Thursday about 2 of the Clock in the afternoone came Doctor *Richard* Bentley (the then New Master,) to Trinity College, and was in the Chappell the same afternoone admitted and sworne Master of Trinity College, in the roome of Doʳ John Mountagu (late Master) now made Deane of Durham.

1ˢᵗ February Doʳ Bentley Maʳ of Trin. Coll.

[1700]

Mʳ Robt Drake senior dyed at London, this being Munday.

22 July Mʳ Drake Senʳ dyed

Dyed Alderman Isaac Watlington about 12 or one of the clock *at noone or afternoone*, on Thursday and buryed in Great Sᵗ Maryes Church on the Tuesday following being the 29ᵗʰ October 1700.

24 Oct. Mʳ Watlington dyed

[170⁰⁄₁]

Mʳˢ Susanna Barnes wife of Doctor Miles Barnes dyed, this Saturday night, her funerall was on Sunday night the 30ᵗʰ March 1701 at Sᵗ Andrewes Church.

22 March Doʳ Barnes's wife dyed

[1701]

31ᵗʰ March Mʳˢ Crabb Alderman Crabbs 2ᵈ wife dyed being
Mʳ Aldⁿ Crabb dyed   Munday night.

[170½*]

March 8ᵗʰ Sunday King Wᵐ dyed   This morning about *4* 8 of the Clock dyed King William the 3ᵈ at *Kensington* and on the same day was the Princesse Anne of Denmarke proclaimed at London Queene, *and at Cambridge by the Maior Aldermen &c on Tuesday the 10ᵗʰ March 1701 about 3 in the afternoone, and by the University about 2 in the same afternoone, and by the Sheriffe and Countrey at Cambridge and Cambridge Castell on Thursday the 12ᵗʰ March 1701.*

A Copy of Sir John Cottons Letter to mee from London.

March 9, 1701

Sir,

Sunday morning a little after eight the King died, Saturday in the evening he sent to the Lord Chief Justice to make his Will, which was finisht about twelve, at that time being a little drousie, he tryed to sleep, but it being in vaine, at 4 he call'd for his Will, and signed it, then for the Lord of Canturbury, from whome he received the Sacrament, and pray'd for the people of England, and advised them to unite against the Common Enemy, He told the Lord Portland he had *been* allwayes a good servant to him and he thank't him for it, He spoak to the Lord of Albermarle to take the Keyes of His Closett, and strong box out of his pockett, and take care of his Papers, He askt his Duch Doctor what he thought of him, he said he thought him in very great danger, then the clock stroke, he said it was seven, the Lord of Canterbury came to his

* Mʳ Benj: Young Maior 1701 & 1702.

bedside, he told him he would speak to him if he could, and immediately shrinks into the bed and dies in one of his bedchambers men armes, the Lord Overkirk son died away, for sometime, in the Kings chamber, which gave him some disturbance; Queene Anne was proclaimed about 3 by the unanimous consent of both Houses, and addresses are ordered to be drawen upp, and when the Lords went in the morning to kisse her hand, shee told them shee desired to raigne noe longer then she putt the Lawes in Execution both in Church and State.

   I am Sir Your assured friend and servant
            J. COTTON.

To Alderman Newton at his
  house in Cambridge.

[1702*]

 Sunday night about 11 of the clock dyed Dr James Ayloffe *Fellow of the College* at his Lodgeings in Trinity Hall, and was buryed Tuesday night 5 May 1702 in the Middle Chancell of St Edwards Church. *3 May. D^r Ja. Ayloffe dyed.*

 I Samuel Newton in the afternoone at the Rose Taverne in Cambridge was sworne Justice of the Peace for the Towne of Cambridge by John Pyke Towne Clarke by vertue of a Dedimus Mr Jeffery the Attorney being then present, And the same time with me were sworne Justices for the said Towne Mr Benjamin Young then Mayor, Mr Thomas Ewin, Mr Thomas Fox and Mr Thomas Fowle sen^r. Aldermen, this was upon the renewing the Commission for the Peace, and wee all then tooke the usuall Oathes for Justices. *24 August Munday Barthol. day*

    * Mr Benj. Young Mayor.

·C. A. S. Octavo Series. XXIII.   8

[1703]

21 Mar.
Dr Stoyt dyed

Doctor Edward Stoyt dyed about 2 of the Clock this afternoone being Sunday aged 86 yeares and upwards, being in the 87th year of his age and buryed on Thursday following.

The 26 Nov. windy storme

Fryday night and Saturday morning till break of day hapned and continued a most terrible and dreadfull storme of winde, with some lightning, much endamaged many houses and places and killed by the fall of chimneyes and buildings much people *and particulerly the Bishopp of Bath and Wells and his Lady killed upon the fall of part of his dwelling house.*

[170$\frac{3}{4}$]

6 March Mr Worts dyed

Munday dyed Mr William Worts one of the Esquire Beadles of this University betweene the houres of 7 and 9 at night, and buryed in Great St Maryes Church on the Fryday following being the 10th March 1703 betweene 6 and 9 at night.

3 July 1705 Mrs Worts dyed

Tuesday dyed Mrs Mary Worts wife of the said Mr William Worts and was buryed in Great St Maryes Church the Saturday following the 7th July 1705.

Mr William Worts Her son dyed on Commencement Sunday morning 3 July 1709.

[1704]

10 April Alderm. Lawson dyed

Munday about 12 of the clock dyed Alderman Thomas Lawson at the Brewhouse in St Andrewes Parish late Mr Rixes.

[170$\frac{4}{5}$]

17 Febr. Mr Flack dyed

Saturday morning dyed Mr Robert Flack at his dwelling house in Linton.

Daniel Love Gent. Mayor.

[1705]
16 April

Tuesday On *Munday* sometime after 12 a clock came Queene *Anne* to Cambridge, and was met by the Corperacion of the Towne on Christs College Peece and after a speech made by Sir John Cotton Baronet our Recorder was conducted from thence by Mr *Mayor* my Lord Oxford our High Steward and the rest of the Corporacion to the Regent Walk, the Common Councell this time rid on horseback, which was not formerly done, at the Regent Walk we left her: The Duke of Somerset then Chancellour of the Vniversity and Master of the Horse was then here, and performed his place as Chancellour, the Vice Chancellour (Dr *John Ellis*) not then appearing as Vice Chancellor for that day

Queen Anne came to Cambr. Dr John Ellis then Vice-Chancellor, then Ma^r of Gonv. & Caius Coll

The same day, the Queene Knighted Do^r Ellis.

Mr James Fletcher
    Maior

[1706*]

Mr *James* Thompson son of Anthony Thompson Esquire at a private Common day holden on this Thursday was sworne a free Burgesse of the Corperacion of Cambridge.

18 July

Saturday Welbore Ellis Doctor in Divinity and Bishopp of Kildare in Ireland was on this day marryed to the daughter of Sir John Briscoe Knight living in Northamptonshire.

20th July B^{pp} of Kildare marryed.

Thursday Mr James Fletcher Maior of Cambridge a little before 9 of the clock in the Evening of that day departed this life, and on Sunday following the 11th of August 1706 was buryed in St Andrewes Churchyard, Mr Washington Minister of Little St Maryes preacht his funerall Sermon his text was the 40 Psalm 1. 2. I waited patiently for the Lord &c. Mr Thomas Fox jun^r on the 10th August 1706 was chosen Mayor in his roome till Michaelmas following.

8th Aug. Mr James Fletcher Mayor dyed

* Mr James Fletcher Mayor 1706

Fryday
9 Aug
Mr Tho
Fox Junr
elected
Maior the
10th Aug

Mr Ewin, Mr Fox sen^r and Mr Fowle sen^r came to my house to me to consult with me *together with Mr Towne Clerk* what was necessary to be done, uppon the death of Mr Fletcher for chusing of a Mayor in his roome for the remainder of his year, and having considered and perused the *old* Common day book what had bin formerly done in the like case, wee concluded that a Common day should be summoned to bee on the next morning at 9 of the clock to Elect a Mayor, and accordingly notice was then given *to the Aldermen Common Councell &c* by the Serjeants. At which time wee met at the Hall, There was then present Sir John Cotton, our Recorder, Mr Welbore deputy Recorder And of the Aldermen my selfe, Mr Ewin, Mr Fox sen^r, Mr Fowle sen^r, Mr Chambers, Mr Frohock Mr Love, Mr Fox jun^r, Mr Fowle jun^r and Mr Peircy. At which Common day Mr Thomas Fox junior by the 18 Electors* (which were all sworne) was chosen Mayor for the remayning part of Mr Fletchers year to Michaelmas next and he was sworne accordingly, and then the Vice Chancellour (Dr Balderston deputy) and 2 Proctors Mr Stephens and Mr Clutterbuck gave him their oath as is usuall. But Mr Love haveing bin appointed by Mr Fletcher his deputy Mayor and by that meanes having then in his hands the Mace *which* being demanded *in the Hall* by the new Mayor to deliver the same to him refused soe to doe, But *for all that* of his owne Accord in the Evening of the same Saturday he sent the Great Mace by Cole one of the Serjeants unto Mr Fox jun^r on that day chosen Mayor for the remaining part of Mr Fletchers year. Mr Alderman Love would have continued Deputy Maior till Michaelmas *next* as Mr Fletchers deputy but it would not be permitted.

* All of the Electors that were then present in the Hall that were *formerly* of Mr Fletchers election together with others by them then chosen to make upp the number of 18 were now the electors of this election for Mr Fox Junr Mayor.

Tewesday in the Evening Dr Thomas Browne Master of Pembroke Hall by his man sent to speak with me, to whome I then *soone* went, who tould me that he sent for me (I being as then a......ed Registrar of that College) to attest (as then I understood) what the College had determined concerning Mr Tudwayes place as Organist of that College, which was then (*at my being there*) writ in a book they then there had; to This effect *that* *writing being* Dated (as I take it on or about the 24 July last) That whereas the said Mr Tudway had spoken some words that highly reflected on Her Majestie therefore they did deprive him of his said place of Organist of the said College, To which said writing in the said book, in my presence the said master Dr Thomas Browne and Mr Thomas Thomas and Mr Ashbourne (*I think* Treasurers of the said College), did then write their names, and after that I did read out of the said book the said determinacion (to the words thereof therein written I refer my selfe) and they did severally (upon my asking them) acknowledge the same, To which I was desired by them to sett my hand as witnes thereof: And to which I writt thus, Attested by Samuel Newton Registrar Coll.

13th Aug Mr Tho. Tudway put out his Organists place at Pembr Hall*

Fryday being a generall Common day, On which day in the 1st *place* was Mr William Rumbold Vintner elected Alderman in the roome of Mr Fletcher lately deceased. Afterwards on the Same day was chosen Mr Thomas Fowle junior New Elect to be Mayor for the ensueing year.

16th Aug Mr Tho. Fowle Jun. New Elect

[1707†]

Saturday night about 10 or 11 at the Rose Taverne in Cambridge upon a quarrell betweene Alderman Thomas Fox junr. & Joseph Pyke concerning the Towne Clarks

19 April Mr Fox junr stab'd Joseph Pyke

* And in March or begin of Apr 1707 by Her Maties favour and by intercession made for him was restored againe to his former places he first making before the University a formall and publique recantacion for what he had said.

† Mr Thos. Fowle jun^r. Maior.

place, the said Mr Fox with his penknife did stabb the said Joseph Pyke in his side near his belly; *but he recovered of the wound.*

26 April my Fall

Saturday morning about 10 a clock, I then coming from Mr Millers Chamber in Trinity College fell downe 4 or 5 staires stopping against *a* Wall which fall was very dangerous to mee, my head a little broke and bruised, and my side much pain'd, but through Gods great mercy (for which I blesse and praise his most holy name) noe bone broken.

30th May Towne Clark Mr Pyke dyed.

Friday about 10 of the Clock in the morning Dyed Mr John Pyke the Towne Clark and buryed in St Edwards Church the 3d June 1707 being Tuesday at the Upper end of the south Chancell next the East Wall,

30th May Bpp of Ely dyed

Fryday dyed Dr Symon Patrick Bishopp of Ely.

23 October Dr Cook dyed

Thursday dyed Dr William Cook Fellow of Jesus College in Cambridge Chauncelor of the Bishopp and Archdeacons Ecclesiastical Courts.

[170$\frac{7}{8}$]

29 Janry

Thursday morning after 2 of the clock I dreamed, methought I digged my owne Grave, but I said this is not deep enough, and some body els (I know not who) digg'd it deeper, but he digg'd it as much too deep, and at one end of it, it by a prety big hole broke through into a long place or floor like to a malting floor, and me thought I went from thence into an old little roome near the said grave, and there was my coffin the topp being not on, *it was* a very plain Coffin, and old Mr Lawson the shoomaker was there driving in small nayels upon leather at the bottome of the Coffin round about the Coffin, to keep corrupcion from issueing out, and me thought I said (I know not to whome) I am alive, I will not be buryed alive, stay till I am dead; Lord I pray the fitt and prepare mee for the houre of my death.

* Mr Thomas Foule Junr. Mayor.

Alderman Daniel Love dyed in the morning being Saturday about one or 2 of the clock. — 6th March

Paid 18s. in my Son's presence unto Mr Edward Wrangle of Fenditton for 200 of billetts and ½ a 100 of faggots, each at 6s. per °, to be delivered next Munday morning, which were delivered accordingly. — 6 march

Tuesday was the first day Gillman Walles went into Pembroke Hall to continue there and was the first night he lodged in the College. — 23 March

[1708]

Hock Tuesday Mr Peter Betson was chose Alderman, in the roome of Mr Daniel Love Alderman deceased, who then accepted of it and was then sworne as is usuall. — 20 April

Mr *William* Rumbold Vintner (being Munday) was chose New Elect, and *at Michaelmas following sworne Mayor.* — 16 Aug.

Thursday dyed His Royall Highnes George Prince of Denmark. — 28 October Prince George dyed

[170 8/9 †]

Munday afternoone dyed Mr Thomas Foule senior Alderman, and buryed in Great St Maryes Church in the North Isle on Sunday following being the 16th of January 1708. — 10 January Mr Foule senr dyed

Heeretofore   The Citizens of London obteined to be governed by Bayliffs, whereas before time they were governed by Portgreeves, The Chief Magistrate or Ruler of the City of London, in the time of holy King Edward the Confessor was named thus

    Wolgarius } Portgreve

In the time of William Conquerour and William Rufus
    Godfrey de Magnum } Portgreve
    Roce de Parc } Provost

In the time of King Henry the First
    Hugh Bothe } Portgreve   Leosianus } Provost

---

* Mr Tho. Fox Senr. Mayor 1707 & 1708 the 3d time.

† Mr William Rumbold Mayor 1708 & 1709.

After them
> Albericus de Veri } Portgreve } Ro. Barquerell } Provost

In the time of King Stephen
> Gilbert Becket } Portgreve Andrew Buchuint } Provost

In the time of Henry the Second
> Peter fitz'Walter } Portgreve

After him
> John fitz'Nigeily } Portgreve

After him
> Ernulph Buchel } Portgreve

The first Bayliffes in the time of King Richard the First Anno Domini 1190.
> Henry Cornehill } Bayliffes
> Richard Remery }

And soe the Chief Governours of the City went by the name of Bayliffes to the 9th year of King John 1208
> Roger Winchester } Anno 9 King John 1208
> Edmund Hardell } Bayliffes

These were the last Bayliffes, afterwards the City was governed by a Maior and Sheriffes.

The First Mayor of London in the 10th year of King John 1209 — This year was granted to the Cittizens of London, by the Kings Letters Patents, that they should yearly chose to themselves a Maior and two Sheriffes. The Sheriffes doe enter on the 28th of September, the Mayor doth enter on the 28th of October next following.

> The first Sheriffes of London { Peter Duke } 28 September Sheriffes 1209
> { Thomas Neale }
>
> The first Mayor of London { Henry fitz' Alwyne } 28 October Mayor 1209

1209 London Bridge built with stone — This year began the Arches of London Bridge to be builded with stone by the worthy Merchants Serle Mercer, and William Alman and Bennit Botewrith. vide Stowes Chronicle.

Saturday morning about 7 of clock dyed Mr Philip
Reynolds 2d Butler of St Johns College He died of a fall he
had the day before in Allhallowes Churchyard against one
of the Church Butrises broke his shoulder bone and bruised
his body, he was just before he fell taken with a sweeming
in his head. He was buryed the Tuesday night following in
St Buttolphs Church.

19 March Phil. Reynolds dyed

Friday at an adjourned generall Common *day* in the
roome of Alderman Thomas Foule senr. lately deceased was
Mr Joseph Pyke chosen Alderman who accepted thereof and
was then sworne.

18 March Jos. Pyke chose Alderman

[1709*]

Sunday morning about 7 a clock (Commencement Sunday) dyed Mr William Worts son of Mr William Worts the
Esquire Beadle deceased and was buryed on Fryday night
following the 8th of July 1709 in the North Isle of Great
St Maryes Church.

3 July Mr Worts dyed

Munday dyed Alderman Nicholas Eagle betweene 5 and
6 a clock in the Evening and buryed Thursday night following the 7th July 1709 on the Northside of St Clements
Churchyard.

4 July Alderm Eagle dyed

Tuesday Mr Francis Piercey was chosen New Elect.

16 Aug

Mr John Carrington, was chosen Alderman in the roome
of Mr Nic. Eagle lately deceased

16 Aug

the same day Mathew Martin was chosen a Common
Counselman in room of Mr Day deceased.

[1710]

Dr Roderick Provost of Kings College Vice Chancellour.

Saturday morning dyed at London Doctor [George]
Brampston Master of Trinity Hall in Cambridge
and in his roome was elected in Midsomer week 1710 Sir

3 June Dr Brampston dyed

---

* Mr Francis Percy Mayor 1709 & 1710.

Nathanael Lloyd Master, who that week took his degree of Doctor of the Civil Law.

<small>20 June Mr Bendyshe dyed</small>

Tuseday night about 10 a Clock at night dyed Thomas Bendyshe Esquire at his dwellinghouse in Marleborough street in Westminster, And on Fryday the 23 June 1710 about 5 or 6 a clock in the afternoone brought downe and buryed in Barrington Church *in a little Chappell there.*

<small>3 July Lady Hatton died</small>

Munday in the afternoon about 2 a Clock Dyed the Lady   Hatton at Long Stanton wife to Sir Christopher Hatton Baronet; and she was buryed there on Fryday following the 7th July 1710.

<small>5^t October</small>

Thursday, without any opposition Hind John Cotton Esq and Samuel Sheapherd Esq were unanimously Elected Burgesses for this Corporacion to sitt in the ensueing Parliament

<small>5^t Oct.</small>

in the afternoone for the University were Elected for their Burgesses of Parliament the Honble Mr Windesor and Dr Paske Fellow of Clare Hall. They were opposed by Mr Shaw of St Johns Colledge, and Mr Gill of Jesus Colledge, both of them haveing formerly bin Fellow Commoners in their respective Colledges.

<small>10 Oct.</small>

1^{lb} 7^s 0^d for 16 yards and a half of lace at 20^d a yard for my new Auditors Gowne paid itt to Mr Herri[ng].

<small>15 Novemb^r Alderman Fox Senr dyed</small>

Wednesday night about Eleaven a Clock dyed Alderman Thomas Fox sen^r and was buryed on the Sunday following being the 19th November 1710 in an Apartment next the Chancell of the Parish Church of All Saints in Cambridge.

[1711†]

<small>27 March Dr Gowarth dyed</small>

Tuseday about 12 a clock at noone dyed at St John's Colledge Lodgeing Dr Humphrey Gowerth *or Goward* Master of St John's, Lady Margaret's Professor of the Uni-

---

* M^r Fr. Percy Mayor.
† Mr Joseph Pyke Mayor 1710–1711.

versity, Prebendary of Ely and Rector of Fen-ditton and was buryed in that College Chappell on   the
of Aprill 1711.

John *Samuel* Shepherd Esquire in the year of the said Mʳ Pykes maioralty at his charges caused our great Town Mace to be made soo great as now it is, it being before much smaller.

Wednesday, According to the printed Picture I then saw, and the descripcion therein given One Jane Scrimshaw the daughter of Thomas Scrimshaw Wooll Stapler born in London in the Parish of Sᵗ Mary le Bow 1584 April the 3ᵈ she is alive and Healthy this Present   1711 At the Marchant Taylors Alms House on Little Tower Hill, This Picture is done by the life. 4ᵗʰ April

She is full pretty round face, pictured in her hat of a *high Crowne* sugarloaf fashion steeple crown something broad brim, with a hood tyed under her chin, a hansome whisk *or band* about her shoulders, white apron and foresleeves, Aged at this time 127 yeares.

Saturday its reported that dyed of the Small Pox at the Lady Hewitts at   Mʳ   Clarke Fellow of Clare Hall and one of the Esquire Beadles of this Vniversity of Cambridge *This was false report, he is recovered and very well in health.* 5ᵗʰ May he dyed not but recovered

On Fryday Died Mʳˢ   Gillman the mother of Mʳ Charles Gilman Apothecary. She sickened on the Munday and dyed on the Fryday following. May

Mʳ Joseph Pyke then Mayor on *Wednesday* was burnt in the mouth supposing it a Cancer in his mouth. May

Saturday Mʳ Edward Chapman and Mʳˢ Sarah Halfhyde the daughter of Mʳ Edmund Halfhyde Apothecary were marryed at London. 28 July

Dʳ Wright Arrabick Professer Dyed at Cambridge And buried at Linton 16 Nov. 1711. 13 Nov.*

Mʳ Sanderson a blind man chosen Mathematick Professer in the roome of Mʳ Whiston who was expell'd the 20 Nov.

* Mʳ John Carrington Mayor.

University for mainteyning the Arian Error contrary to the Doctrine of the Church of England.

[1712]

26 March
Dr Roderick dyed & buryed

Wednesday about one of the clock that morning dyed Dr Charles Roderick Doctor in Divinity Provost of Kings Colledge in Cambridge, Dean of Ely and Rector of Milton, And on Tuseday following being the 1st of April 1712 before 6 in the afternoon he was buryed in Kings College Chappell within the Little Chappel, there leading into that College Library; He left a wife and 2 children behind him a son and a daughter.

7th April
A new Provost Dr Adams then chosen Provost by the College

Munday morning in the room of Dr Roderick deceased was chosen for Provost of Kings College in Cambridge Dr John Adams Doctor in Divinity,

the first time after, that he came to Cambridge was on Thursday the 1st day of May 1712 between 3 and 4 in that afternoone, and was on Fryday the day following the 2d of May 1712 Admitted Provost of the Kings College in Cambridge.

4th of May
Dr Tindale dyed

On Sunday morning about 2 of the clock Dyed *William* Tindale of Trinity Hall Doctor in *Divinity* *Law* Minister of St Edwards Parish in Cambridge

and was buryed on Saturday following being the 10th May 1712 between the North and Middle Chauncell of St Edwards Church at the upper end thereof.

21th May
Dor Syke

Wednesday Morning Dr [H.] Syke a German, of Trinity College in Cambridge and Hebrew Professor of the Vniversity, was found dead in his Chamber uppon the Floore, haveing hanged himselfe with his Girdle or shash which he girded himself in his morning Gowne, but with his weight, the girdle had broke, the other part thereof had throatled and strangled him, he was the night before in the College Hall at Supper and eat Sperragrasse, he was this morning to have gone to London with Mr Crownfield a Printer, who

* 1711 & 1712 Mr John Carrington Mayor.

came this morning betimes to call him, but finding his dore shutt, and noe answer made uppon his much knocking, feared all was not right and soe caused the dore to be broke ope, which done, he was found dead on the Floor, he was observed for some time lately to be melancholy.

Fryday This morning in Hyde Park was fought a duell between Duke Hamilton and the Lord Mohone both killed Mohone upon the spot and the Duke being carryed home dyed within few houres. *14 November*

Munday *Sunday night and* this morning *being Munday the 17th November* 1712 and the last night was a very strong West winde, and in it at Bottisham hapned a violent fire which burnt down and consumed many houses as it was commonly reported above 20. This fire began on 16 November 1712 being Sunday about 9 at night. **17* 16 November*

Munday morning at Chesterton Church was marryed Mr Samuel Burton a Fellow Commoner of Trinity Hall to Mrs Susanna Fox the daughter of old Alderman Thomas Fox deceased *17th November*

And on Sunday night about 10 of the Clock being the 30h of November 1712 he dyed at Chesterton, he was very ill when he maryed.

[17 12/13]

Samuel Gatward Esquire was elected Recorder of Cambridge in the room of Sir John Cotton Bart deceased It was on Tuesday an adjourned Common day from Twelf Common day, And on the same day he was also chose Conservator of the River in room of Sir John Cotton deceased. *17 Janry Mr Gatwd*

[1713]

Sunday morning dyed Dr [Samuel] Blyth master of Clare Hall and buryed on Thursday night 23 April 1713 in the South Chancell in St Edwards Church. *19 April*

Fryday at 2 *in the afternoone* was the Peace between Great Brittain and France proclaimed on horseback by the *8 May*

<small>Peace with France proclaimed</small> Mayor and Aldermen in Scarlet and Common Councell in their Gownes, The Mayor having this day received a Proclamacion with a Writt annexed for that purpose,

the proclamacion was read by Alderman Fox Towneclark and spoke or repeated more audibly by Daniel Aires the Serjeant, proclaimed first at the Market Cross, and then at severall other places in the Towne.

[1714]

Mr Thomas Jermin then Mayor.

1st August   Sunday morning about 7 a clock Queen Anne dyed.

On the same day at London was the High and mighty Prince, George Elector of Brunswick-Lunenburgh proclaimed King of Great Britain France and Ireland.

3 August   Tuesday in the afternoon He was proclaimed both by the University and by the Town of Cambridge proclaimed King George.

18 September   Saturday about 6 in the afternoone King George with His son Prince George came from Holland by Sea and landed at Greenwich And on Munday the 20th September 1714 they by Land made their publike entrie to London by Southwarke and soe through London and Westminster to St James's to which place they arrived between 6 and 7 at night. King George his Coronation was on Wednesday the 20th of October 1714.

10th December   On Thursday night dyed Mr John Cooper Senior Fellow of Trinity College, and was buryed in Trinity College Chappel on Sunday night following being the 13th December 1714.

[171$\frac{4}{5}$]

7th Jan^{ry}   Fryday in the Evening dyed Mr John Perne Esquire Beadle, and on Wednesday the 12th January 1714 was chosen in his place Esquire Beadle M^r   Atwood Fellow of Pembroke Hall.

[1715]

Mr Charles Chambers
Mayor the 2^d time.

Fryday morning, between 9 and 10 was an Ecclipse of the Sun, it was so dark I could not see to goe but was led by my Cosin William Fuller from about his shopp as far as the 3 Tunns. and then it began to be light the great darknes continued hardly a quarter of an houre. 22 April

Tuesday about 2 a clock in the afternoone dyed Alderman John Frohock at the Bull in Bishopsgate street in London after 5 weekes lyeing there wounded and sick by meanes of a Candle got by chance hold of his neckcloath and cloathes burning him in a very sore manner And was buryed on the Fryday night following being the 3^d of June 1715 in the Church of   near Bishopsgate London. 31 May
Ald^{rm} Frohock dyed

Thursday about 2 a clock afternoon dyed at Cottenham Doctor   Smith Rector of that Church and Prebendary of Ely and was buryed on Saturday following the 11th June 1715 at Cottenham. 9th June

On Thursday morning about 9 a clock Dyed my Cosin Susanna Jones widow at her dwelling house in Westminster, and buried at Amersden in 7th July
Cosin Jones dyed

Munday Evening dyed Mrs Mary Whitlock widow at Trumpington, Aged about 87 yeares, and buryed there, on Thursday 8th Sept. 1715. 5th Sept*

[1716]

On Monday Dyed Doctor John Edwards. 16th April

Munday about 10 in the morning dyed Mr Hugh Martin Esquire Bedle and *was* buryed on the Wednesday night following in St Edwards Church further north Chancell being the 8th of August 1716. 6th Aug.
Mr Martin Beadle dyed

* Mr Thomas Fox Mayor.

10th Aug	Fryday M`r` Robert Simpson Fellow of Caius College was chosen Esquire Beadle in the roome of M`r` Martin deceased.
10 Aug	M`r` Boston had then given him the Wine License.
16 Aug.	At a Common day, chose into the roome of Alderman John Frohock deceased M`r` Wilson, and M`r` Randall Alderman into the roome of M`r` Peircy Alderman deceased And after he was sworne Alderman the same Common Day he resigned his Aldermans place, and in the roome of him was chosen Alderman, M`r` Whiskin on Bartholomew day the 24 August 1716.
16 Aug M`r` Wilson New Elect	was chosen New Elect for Mayor M`r` Wilson and sworn Mayor The 29 September 1716.
29 Sept.	on Saturday Do`r` Christopher Anstey marryed to M`rs` Mary Thompson daughter of Anthony Thompson Esq.

[1717†]

12th June M`r` Dent dyed	Wednesday morning about 6 of the clock dyed M`r` Peter Dent.

* M`r` Thomas Fox Mayor.
† M`r` John Wilson Maior.

INDEX.

Adams, John, elected Bailiff, 2; High Constable, 25; Alderman, 28

Adams, Dr John, elected Provost of King's College, 124

Albemarle, George Duke of, death, 55

Alders, James, Freeman, 35

Alexander, James, marries Margery Musson, 110

Alington, Hildebrand, Freeman, 64

Alington, William Lord, death and burial of, 87

Allen, son of Alderman, Freeman, 49

Alman, William, commences London Bridge, 120

Almshouses in St Clement's Parish, Lease of, 49

Anne, Queen, proclaimed in Cambridge, 112; visits Cambridge, 115; death of, 126

Anstey, Dr Christopher, marries Mrs Mary Thompson, 128

Apprentices, Registration of, 43

Artereall, Michael, teaches Alderman Newton's son French, 80

Assizes, 10, 17, 32, 42, 62

Atkinson, Troylus, Bookseller, death of, 74

Attwood, Mr, Fellow of Pembroke, elected Esquire Bedell, 126

Audit, Town, 10

Auditor, at Trinity College, his fees, allowances, &c., 54, 55

Aungier, John, appointed Clerk of Gt St Mary's, 17

Austin, Cornelius, elected Treasurer, 26

Ayloffe, James, baptized, 24

Ayloffe, Dr James, Fellow of Trinity Hall, death and burial of, 113

Ayloffe, William, Fellow of Trinity College, elected Public Orator, 110

Babington, Dr Humfrey, Vice-Master of Trinity, sudden death of, 106

Baden, Andrew, keeps his first Act for M.D., 110

Bagley, Mr, Curate of Barnwell, death of, 12

Bailiffs of the City of London, 120

Bainbridge, Mary, Relict of Dr Bainbridge, Master of Christ's, death and burial of, 59

Baldero, Dr, preaches sermon at St Edward's Church, 38

Balls, Freeman, 51

Barnes, Mr, Peterhouse, Proctor, 27

Barnes, Susanna, wife of Dr Miles Barnes, death and burial of, 111

Barnwell Abbey, Mayor and Aldermen at, 27, 48

Baron, William, elected Town Clerk, 72

Barquerell, R., Provost of London, 120

Barrow, Dr Isaac, Master of Trinity

C. A. S. Octavo Series. XXIII.

College, arrives in Cambridge, 70; death of, 75

Barton, Francis, Fellow of Trinity College, dies from a fall down stairs, 72

Basset, Joshua, appointed Master of Sidney College, 90

Beaumont ( ), daughter of Dr Beaumont, Master of Peterhouse, dies from Small Pox, 72

Becket, Gilbert, Portreeve of the City of London, 120

Bedford, The Irish reported to have burnt the town and massacred the people at, 97

Bedford, Earl of, elected a free Burgess, and sworn Recorder, 104

Belke, Dr, of Queen's College, reported likely to become Master, 74

Bell, Robert, Pinder, 46

Bendyshe, Thomas, dies in Westminster; his body taken to Barrington, 122

Bennet, Sir Levinus, chosen representative at the Westminster Convention, 97

Bentley, Dr Richard, appointed Master of Trinity College, 111

Berry, Richard, elected Justice of the Peace and Alderman, 93

Betson, Peter, elected Alderman, 119

Bever, John, married to Susanna Bowes, 89

Bird, John, Bailiff, 2

Bird, John, Executor of Thomas Rippington's Will, 25

Bird, John, elected Chief Constable, 32

Bishops committed to the Tower, 94; acquitted, 95

Blackerby, Thomas, vacates the Office of High Constable, 25

Blackley, bound over for breach of the Peace, 49

Blackley, John, elected Councillor, 93

Blackley, Matthew, elected Treasurer, 43, 53; Mayor, 92

Bland, Thomas, elected Councillor, 94

Bloefeild, Mr, elected Councillor, 11

Blyth, Dr Samuel, Master of Clare Hall, death and burial of, 125

Bodenham, Mrs, death and burial of, 67

Boldero, Dr, Vice - Chancellor, preaches the sermon at Gt St Mary's, May 29, 1669, 47

— see Baldero

Boston, Mr, receives a Wine License, 128

Botewrith, B., commences London Bridge, 120

Bothe, Hugh, Portreeve of the City of London, 119

Bottisham, Fire at, 125

Botwright, John, death and burial of, 46

Boyden, elected Treasurer, 26

Boyle, Mr, elected M.P. for the University, 106

Brady, Dr, Master of Caius College, gives order to receive John Newton into the Grammar School, 17

Brakenbury, Dr, St John's College, death of, 106

Brampston, Dr George, Master of Trinity Hall, dies at London, 121

Brand, Thomas, Bailiff, 2

Brattle, Dr Daniel, Senior Fellow of Trinity College, death of, 108

Bretton, Dr, Master of Emmanuel, Speech to the members of the Paving Leet, 61

Brookbank, Dr, Candidate for the representation of the University, 106

Browne, Thomas, Clerk of Gt St Mary's, death of, 17

Browne, Thomas, elected Master of Pembroke College, 107

INDEX.

Bryan, Alderman William, death of, 109
Bryan, Mrs, death and burial of, 105
Buchel, Ernulph, Portreeve of the City of London, 121
Buchuint, Andrew, Provost of London, 120
Buck, John, Esquire Bedell, death of, 81
Buck, Martin, Apothecary, death and burial of, 91
Buck, Thomas, Lease granted to, 51
Buck, Thomas, Esquire Bedell, death and burial of, 56
Buck, Thomas, *jun.*, death and burial of, 95
Buckingham, George Duke of, elected Chancellor of the University, 60
Bumpstead, Charles, elected Councillor, 94
Burton, Samuel, Fellow Commoner of Trinity Hall, marries Mrs Susanna Fox, 125; death of, 125
Butler, William, marriage of, 106
Byng, John, of Grantchester, brings action for forgery against Thomas Terry, 17; death of, 45

Cambridge, rejoicings at the Proclamation of Charles II., 1; Comet, 7, 12; Audit, 10; Assizes, 10, 17, 32, 42, 62; Fast Day on account of the Dutch war, 11; Do. on account of the Plague, 15; deaths from the Sickness, 15; fiery appearance of the sky, 16; Tempest, 16; Death of Matthew Wren, Bp of Ely, the body brought to Cambridge and buried in Pembroke College Chapel, 18—20; Quarter Sessions, 25, 32, 40, 49, 60; allowances made to the Mayor for the proposed visit of the King and Queen, 34; Alderman Moodey sent by the Corporation to provide presents for them, 34; their plans are changed and they do not visit Cambridge, 35; the Town Clerk required to make a Catalogue of all books and writings in his hands, 39; The King's Fast Day, 40; arrival of the Prince of Tuscany, 43; his reception by the University and Town, 44, 45; celebration of the birth and return of Charles II., 46, 47; visit of the Duke and Duchess of York and others, 57, 58; visit of the Prince of Orange, 58; arrival of Charles II., his reception, &c., 64; visit of the Duchess of York, 79, 80; arrival of the Morocco ambassador, 82, 83; Proclamation of James II., 88; address to the King, 88, 89; bonfire on Market Hill to celebrate the birth of the Prince of Wales, 94; the disbanded Irish reported to be on their way here, and great uproar in consequence, 96, 97; Proclamation of William and Mary, 98—101; arrival of William III., his reception, 103, 104; earthquake shock, 106; Proclamation of Queen Anne, 112; visit of Queen Anne, 115; Peace proclaimed, 125, 126; George I. proclaimed, 126
Carrington, John, elected Alderman, 121
Castle End, permission granted to the Mayor to plant trees on the waste there, 39
Challis, Francis, elected Treasurer, 26
Chambers, Charles, Mayor, 127
Chaplin, John, elected Councillor, 93
Chapman, Alderman Edward, Mayor,

9—2

2; Deputy Mayor, 7; Auditor, 11; death of, 28; Bequest to the Town, 46, 52

Chapman, Alderman Edward, married, 78; death and burial of, 109

Chapman, Edward, married to Mrs. Sarah Halfhyde, 123

Chapman, Mrs, obtains renewal of a Lease, 49

Charles II., proclaimed King by the Town and University, 1; expected visit of the King and Queen to Cambridge, arrangements for, 34; Alderman Moodey goes to London to procure presents for them, 34; they do not however visit Cambridge, 35; Fast day on account of his sufferings, 40; celebration of his birth and return, at Cambridge, 46, 47; his Crown, Sceptre, &c., stolen from the Tower, 60; visits Cambridge, 64; his reception by the Town and University, 65, 66; at Newmarket when the fire broke out there, 84; illness, death, and funeral of, 87, 88

Chevin, Alderman Richard, Obit sermon, 6, 9, 41

Chicheley, Sir Thomas, elected High Steward, 59; a representative at the Westminster Convention, 97

Christmas Customs, 7, 38

Church, Richard, appointed Mayor, 85; death, 86

Clare Hall, £100 lent to, by the Town, 52

Clarke, Edmund, death of, 82

Clarke, Mr, Fellow of Clare Hall, false report of his death from Small Pox, 123

Clay, Mr, elected Alderman, 93

Clench, Mr, Mayor, 3

Clench, John, of Bottisham, death of, 42

Coffee, Proclamation forbidding the sale of, 74

Cogey, Nathaniel, Pembroke Coll., preaches sermon at Trinity Church before the Mayor, &c., 3; elected Master, 75; death of, 107

Colbourne, Mr, his goods seized, 103

Cole, John, brother in law of Samuel Newton, death of, 56

Comedy House, 45

Comet, 7, 12, 81, 82

Commencement, 59

Common, Cattle not allowed on the, before May Day, 45

Cook, Dr William, Fellow of Jesus College, death of, 118

Cooke, Peter, elected Councillor, 93

Cooper, John, Bailiff, 2

Cooper, John, Senior Fellow of Trinity College, death and burial of, 126

Copinger, Thomas, Minister of Trumpington, death of, 72

Coplestone, Dr, Provost of King's, death and burial of, 102

Corker, William, Steward of Trinity College, 55

Cornhill, Henry, Bailiff of the City of London, 120

Corporations, Act concerning, 34, 77

Cotton, Sir John, chosen representative at the Westminster Convention, 97; Letter on the death of William III., 112, 113; elected M.P. for Cambridge, 122.

Cotton, Sir Robert, chosen representative at the Westminster Convention, 97

Covell, Dr John, elected Master of Christ's College, 95

Covile, Lewis, Freeman, 53

Crabb, Nathaniel, Treasurer, 2; elected Alderman 3; sends

present to the Mayor, 8; elected Mayor, 29, 32; 86, 93
Crabb, Mrs, mother of Alderman Crabb, death of, 63
Crabb, Mrs, wife of Alderman Crabb, death and burial of, 78
Crabb, Mrs, Alderman Crabb's second wife, death of, 112
Crane, Dr Robert, Fellow of Trinity College, death of, 70
Cranway, James, marriage, 62
Cranwell, John, Auditor of the Church of Ely, 76
Crompton, Mr, Fellow of Jesus College, death of, 108
Cropley, John, Coroner, 33
Cudworth, Dr Ralph, Master of Christ's College, death of, 94
Cullen, Sir Rushet, elected a free Burgess, 104
Cutts, Colonel, elected a free Burgess, 104

Dartmouth, The Dutch land at, 96
Dawes, Sir William, elected Master of St Catharine's, 110
Dawney, Robert, of Norwich, marries Sarah Nicholson, 91
Day, Mrs, wife of Mr T. Day, Apothecary, death of, 79
Dennis, elected Treasurer, 26
Dent, Peter, *sen.*, lease of a piece of waste ground to, 39; death of, 103
Dent, Peter, death of, 128
Dickenson, Mrs, death of, 70
Dickenson, Thomas, elected Councillor, 22
Dickenson, ( ), elected Treasurer, 45
Dillingham, Dr, Master of Clare Hall, death of, 77
Dinners, &c. See Entertainments
Dolphin Inn, 58

Drake, Robert, Coroner, 33; Councillor, 64
Drake, Robert, *sen.*, death of, 111
Duel, 125
Duke, Peter, Sheriff of London, 120
Dunbar, John, death of, 76
Duport, Dr James, Master of Magdalene, preaches sermon at Great St Mary's on the King's Fast Day, 40; elected Vice-Chancellor, 53
Dutch, The, land at Dartmouth, 96
Dutch War, 11, 12

Eachard, Dr John, Master of St Catharine's, death of, 110
Eade, Dr Robert, death of, 67
Eagle, Alderman Nicholas, elected Mayor, 87; death and burial of, 121
Earthquake, 106
Easter Day customs, 11
Eclipse of the Sun, 127
Edward, Dr John, death of, 127
Edwards, Mr., Trinity Lecturer, 41
Ellis, ( ), elected Councillor, 94
Ellis, Dr John, Vice Chancellor, Knighted, 115
Ellis, Samuel, admitted to Trinity College, 46
Ellis, Welbore, Bishop of Kildare, marries a daughter of Sir John Briscoe, 115
Ellis, William, takes his M.A. degree, 59; elected Registrar, and Auditor of Trinity College, 71
Ely, Earthquake in, 106
— fire in, 21
Entertainments, 3, 7, 8, 11, 13, 25, 27, 30, 31, 34, 35, 38, 47, 48, 51, 53, 57, 59, 62, 64, 65, 66, 68, 69, 83, 100, 104, 105
Essex, John, elected Treasurer, 26
Eversden, William, of Eversden, death of, 105

INDEX.

Ewin, Mr, elected Councillor, 11
Ewin, Alderman John, Mayor, 1; Auditor, 11; death and burial of, 26
Ewin, Alderman Thomas, elected Mayor, 105; Justice of the Peace, 113
Executions for murder, &c., 10

Fage, John, elected Mayor and Alderman, 96; Justice of the Peace, 102; death of, 108
Fairbrother, Dr, King's College, death of, 82
Fan, Alderman John, Obit sermon, 5, 37
Fanshaw, Sir Thomas, late M.P. for the University, 17
Fast Days, 11, 15, 40
Felstead, Mr, Treasurer, 11
Felsted, Alderman, resigns, 96
Finch, Francis, elected Mayor, 2
Finch, Griffith, marries Mary Williamson, 6
Fire at Bottisham, 125
— — Ely, 21
— — Newmarket, 84
— — Southwark, 21
— of London, 15, 16
Fish, Proclamation concerning the selling of, 4
Fisher, Dr, chosen Master of St Catharine's, 110
Fishing, 11
Fitz Alwyne, Henry, first Mayor of London, 120
Fitz Nigeily, John, Portreeve of the city of London, 120
Fitz Walter, Peter, Portreeve of the city of London, 120
Flack, Robert, dies at Linton, 114
Fleet at Harwich, 12
Fleetwood, Dr, Provost of King's, elected Vice-Chancellor, 35

Fletcher, James, Mayor, dies during his tenure of Office, 115
Fowle, Thomas, elected Alderman, 77; sworn Justice of the Peace, 87, 113; death and burial of, 119
Fowle, Thomas, *jun.*, elected Mayor, 117
Fox, Thomas, Coroner, elected Treasurer, 26
Fox, Thomas, nominated Lieutenant of the Militia, 104
Fox, Alderman Thomas, marries Susanna Stoyt, 107; a Justice of the Peace, 113; death and burial of, 122
Fox, Thomas, *jun.*, elected Mayor, 115, 116; quarrels with Joseph Pyke and stabs him, 117, 118
Foxton, Mr, Obit sermon, 37
Francis, Father, 90
Frisby, William, Apothecary, death of, 74
Frohock, Anne, death and burial of, 105
Frohock, John, death and burial of, 40
Frohock, John, elected Alderman, 93; death of, 127
Frohock, Margaret, death and burial of, 40
Frohock, Samuel, death and burial of, 42
Frost, Great, 86, 87
Fuller, Robert, elected Bailiff, 13
Fuller, William, elected Councillor, 93
Fullmer, John, death of, 108

Garlick Fair, 21, 51
Gascoigne, Sir Barnard, the Prince of Tuscany's Interpreter, 44
Gatward, Samuel, elected Recorder of Cambridge, 125

INDEX.

George I. proclaimed at Cambridge, 126; his Coronation, 126
George, Prince of Denmark, at Cambridge with William III., 104
Gibbs, Mr, Minister of Great St Mary's, preaches Alderman Herring's funeral sermon, 73
Gibbs, Thomas, Minister of Gt St Mary's, &c., death and burial of, 55
Gilbert, John, elected Councillor, 93
Gill, Mr, Jesus College, a Candidate for the Representation of the University, 122
Gillman, Mrs, death of, 123
Gimbert, Mr, elected Alderman, 93
Gimbert ( ), marries Elizabeth Hawkshaw, 107
Goad, Mrs, death of, 41
Gowarth, Dr, Master of St John's, elected Lady Margaret Professor of Divinity, 94
Gower, Dr Humphrey, Master of St John's College, death and burial of, 122, 123
Graves, Thomas, Butler of Bene't College, sudden death of, 27
Gray, ( ), wife of Samuel, Lease granted to, 52
Greene, Dr Christopher, married at Linton to Mrs Susannah Flack, 98
Greene, Mrs, wife of Dr Chr. Greene, death and burial of, 107
Greswell, Mr, Fellow of Trinity College, killed from a fall down stairs, 8
Griffith, George, Master of the Perse School, death and burial of, 90
Griffith, Thomas, of Trinity College, death of, 71

Hales, Judge, holds the Assizes at Cambridge, 32, 42, 62

Halfhead, Edmund, married to Frances Clerke, 82
Hall, David, Freeman, 45
Halman, Councillor, Deputy Recorder, 60
Hamilton, Duke of, and Lord Mahone, duel between, 125
Hamond, Owen, married to Susannah Rix, 71; death of, 78
Hardell, Edmund, Bailiff of the City of London, 120
Harper, Thomas, Serjeant, 4
Harrow Lane, 38
Hart, Andrew, elected Alderman, 69; death of, 82
Hartcliffe, Mr, Fellow of King's, brings the King's Letters recommending him for the Provostship, 102; B.D. by mandate of the King, 103
Harthorne, Daniel, Porter of Pembroke, death of, 42
Harwich, the Fleet at, 12
Hatton, Lady, death and burial of, at Long Stanton, 122
Hatton, Sir Thomas, Freeman, 64; elected Knight of the Shire, 71; death of, 83
Hawkes, Mr, elected Alderman, 93
Herring, Alderman, Auditor, 11; elected Councillor, 11; Deputy Mayor, receives the Prince of Orange, 58; death and burial of, 73
Herring, Richard, son of Alderman Herring, commits suicide by drowning himself, 37
Hill, Mr, Trinity College, preaches Mrs Wells' funeral sermon, 8
Hinde, Artemus, elected Councillor, 94
Hinton, William, elected Councillor, 28; death and burial of, 75
Hinton, William, his goods seized, 103

136 INDEX.

Hock Tuesday, 12, 26, 43, 93, 119
Holiday, Tom, Town Crier, 45
Howarth, Dr, Master of Magdalene, Vice-Chancellor, 27; death of, 35
Howlett, James, marries Elizabeth Fuller, 110
Hughes, Francis, Esquire Bedell, death and burial of, 53
Hughes, Mr, preaches Alderman Pettit's funeral sermon, 69
Hunt, Captain, Freeman, 59
Hurrell, William, elected Treasurer, 43
Hurry, William, elected Treasurer, 53
Hurst, Roger, seizes the Mayor's goods, 85

Ilger, Alderman John, found dead in bed, 86
Incarsole, Bridget, death of, 59
Irish, The, lately disbanded, reported to be on their way to Cambridge, 96, 97

Jacklyn, John, Town Serjeant, death of, 15
James II. proclaimed King at Cambridge, 88; address from the Town, 88, 89; crosses over to France, 97; reported capture, 99
James, Henry, appointed Master of Queens' College, 74
Jenner, Mr, Sidney College, preaches Alderman Simpson's Funeral Sermon, 24
Jennings, ( ), elected Bailiff, 2, 13; death of, 13
Jerman, Francis, elected Councillor, 24; Mayor, 77
Jermin, Thomas, Mayor, 126
Johnson, Mr, Sidney College, preaches Mrs Crabb's funeral sermon, 78

Jones, Owen, married to Susannah Ellis, cousin of Alderman Newton, 69
Jones, Susanna, Cousin of Alderman Newton, death and burial of, 127

Keeling, *Lord*, Judge at Cambridge Assizes, 9; present from the Mayor and Aldermen to, 9
Kempe, Waldegrave, grant of renewal of a lease to, 51
Kidder, Richard, Bp of Bath and Wells, killed by the fall of chimneys during a storm of wind, 114
King's College, the Prince of Orange dines at the Provost's Lodge, 59
King's College Chapel, Musical entertainment in, 44
Kitchingman, Bryan, Attorney, Death of, 77
Knight of the Shire, polling at the Election of, 71

Law, Edward, Town Clerk, 11; elected Councillor and Alderman, 56; Mayor, 57; resigns his Office of Town Clerk, 72; death of, 75
Lawson, Alderman Thomas, death of, 114
Lee, John, Cook at King's College, death and burial of, 58
Leosianus, Provost of London, 119
Lewis, Dr, Jesus College, death of, 91
Lightfoot, Peter, elected Bailiff, 2, 13; Alderman, 93
Lindsey, John, elected Councillor, 94
Lindsey, Richard, elected Councillor, 93
Lloyd, Sir Nathaniel, elected Master of Trinity Hall, 122
London Bridge begun, 120
—, Earthquake in, 106

INDEX. 137

London, governed by Portreeves, next by Bailiffs, then by the Mayor and Sheriffs, 119, 120
Long, Ralph, elected Councillor, 93
Loosemore, Mr, teaches music to Alderman Newton's son, 77, 78
Love, Daniel, Mayor, 115; death of, 119
Love, Daniel, *jun.*, elected Councillor, 93
Lowry, Thomas, elected Councillor, 93
Lynnett, Dr William, Vice-Master of Trinity College, death and burial of, 111

Mace, Thomas, elected Treasurer, 2; Bailiff, 22
Magnum, Godfrey de, Portreeve of the City of London, 119
Mahone, Lord, and the Duke of Hamilton fight a duel, and are both killed, 125
Mapletoft, Dr Robert, Master of Pembroke College, death of, 75
Market Place, Proclamation concerning the selling of fish, &c. in the, 4
Marsh, Timothy, Serjeant, 4, 5
Marshall, Mr, elected Alderman, 93
Martin, Hugh, elected Esquire Bedell, 81; marries Mrs Mary Simpson, 86; death of, 127
Martin, Matthew, elected Councillor, 121
Martin, Robert, made Butler of Trinity College, 85
Mary, Queen, wife of William III., illness, death and burial of, 108
Mathew, William, marries Anne Beecham, 42
Mathows, William, marries Margaret Mortlock, 70

Matthews, Anne, death of, from small pox, 55
Mayfield, Owen, Auditor, 11; Councillor, 11; Alderman, 56; Mayor, 67; death of, 89
Mayfield, Susanna, daughter of Owen Mayfield, death and burial of, 41
Mayfield, Susannah, daughter of Alderman Mayfield, death and burial of, 105
Mercer, Serle, commences London Bridge, 120
Michaelmas customs, 32
Middleton, ( ), Freeman, 51
Midsummer Fair proclaimed, 48, 61
Militia, 104
Miller, son of Edw. Miller, burial of, 17
Minshall, Dr, Master of Sidney College, death and burial of, 90
Mobile, 96
Monmouth, James Duke of, elected Chancellor of the University, 72
Montagu, Dr John, appointed Master of Trinity College, 85; made Dean of Durham, 111
Moodey, Alderman Samuel, Auditor, 11; sent by the Corporation to London to provide presents for the King and Queen on their proposed visit to Cambridge, 34; resigns his Office of Alderman, 53
Moodey, Samuel, *jun.*, Freeman, 73
Morden, Charles, death and burial of, 101
Morden, Mrs, wife of William Morden, death and burial of, at Ware, 27
More, John, elected Treasurer, 12; Bailiff, 22
More, Dr, Christ's College, death and burial of, 91
More, Mr, of Clare Hall, elected preacher for Sturbridge Fair, 62

Morocco, Ambassador of, visits Cambridge; his reception, 82, 83

Morton, Judge, holds the Assizes at Cambridge, 17

Mosse, Mr, Bene't College, Candidate for the Office of Public Orator, 110

Muriel, Robert, made Butler of Trinity College, 85

Muriell, Alderman Robert, death of, 83

Muryell, Mr, sent to London concerning presents for the King and Queen, 63

Muryell, Thomas, Treasurer, 2

Neach, Mr, Pembroke College, preaches sermon before the Mayor, &c., 52

Neale, Thomas, Sheriff of London, 120

Nelson, (   ), executed for wife murder, 10

Nevill, Clement, oldest Fellow of Trinity College, death and burial of, 85

Newmarket, Fire at, 84

Newton, Isaac, chosen representative at the Westminster Convention, 98; Isaac Newton and the Provostship at King's, 102

Newton, John, son of Alderman Newton, goes to Cambridge Grammar School, 17; apprenticed, 73

Newton, John, son of Alderman Newton's cousin, death and burial of, 105

Newton, Samuel, made a Free Burgess, 2; elected Treasurer, 2; returns from Waterbeach whither he had gone on account of the sickness, 16; his son John Newton first goes to the Grammar School, 17; lease of waste land granted to him, 22; elected a Councillor, 22; illness of his wife, 24; elected Alderman, 28; buys his Aldermanic outfit from the widow of the late Alderman, 29; his entertainment on his appointment, 30; Christmas present to the Mayor, 38; illness, death and burial of his son Samuel, 42, 43; dines with the Mayor, &c., 52; elected Auditor of Trinity College, 53, 54; chosen Mayor, 63; Justice of the Peace, 64, 75, 102, 113; presents sent to him at Christmas, 66; his speech on retiring from the Mayoralty, 68; elected Registrar of Pembroke College, 69; Registrar and Auditor of Trinity College, 71; his son John apprenticed, 73; receives the Sacrament as Justice of the Peace, 76; deputy Mayor, 105; his dreams, 109, 118; his wife breaks her arm, 111; accident to himself, 118

Newton, Samuel, son of Alderman Newton, death of, 43

Newton, Samuel, nephew of Alderman Newton, Freeman, 49

Newton, Samuel, son of Alderman Newton's cousin, baptism of, 98; death of 101

Newton, Samuel, son of Alderman Newton's cousin, burial of, 110

Newton, Samuel, son of Alderman Newton's nephew, baptism and death of, 106

Newton, Samuel, *jun.*, elected Alderman, 86; married to Elizabeth Rogers, 86

Newton, Sarah, cousin of Alderman Newton, death and burial of, 90

Nicholson, Thomas, elected Treasurer, 43

Nightingale, Robert, Singer at King's, death of, 7

INDEX.

Norman, Richard, lease of a slaughterhouse to, 39, 43

North, Dr John, appointed Master of Trinity College, 75; a Justice of the Peace, 76; death of, 85

Northrop, Mr, elected Alderman, 93

Nurse, Mr, Trinity, defeated candidate for Esquire Bedell, 81

Orange, Prince of, visits Cambridge, 58, 59

Orange, Prince and Princess of, 98

Ossory, Lord, 58

Oxendine, Dr, Master of Trinity Hall, elected Vice Chancellor, 106

Page, Sir Thomas, Provost of King's, death and burial of, 82

Paman, Dr, St John's, elected Public Orator, 70

Parc, Roce de, Provost of London, 119

Parliament assembled, 23

Paske, Dr, Fellow of Clare Hall, elected M.P. for the University, 122

Patrick, Simon, Bp of Ely, death of, 118

Patteson, John, Attorney, placed in the Pillory, 10

Paving Leet, 4, 5, 36, 60

Peace between England and France proclaimed at Cambridge, 125, 126

Peachill, Mr, Fellow of Magdalene Coll., preaches Alderman Fan's Obit sermon, 6

Pearson, John, Master of Trinity College, makes Oration at the funeral of Matthew Wren, Bp of Ely, 20; consecrated Bishop of Chester, 70

Pearson, Philip, elected Councillor, 93

Pearson, Richard, elected Councillor, 93

Peck, Mr, St John's College, elected Esquire Bedell, 53

Pedder, William, elected Alderman, 22; death and burial of, 25

Pedder, William, death of, 86

Pembroke Hall, Lease of the Passage into St Tho. Leyes to, 34

Pepys, John, elected Alderman, 96; Justice of the Peace, 102; nominated Captain of the Militia, 104

Pepys, Roger, Recorder of Cambridge, 10; death of, 96

Pepys, Talbot, Freeman, 64

Perne, John, of Peterhouse, elected Esquire Bedell, 85; death of, 126

Perrey. *See* Sterne, Edward

Peters, Thomas, Upholsterer, death and private burial of, 95

Petkins ( ), elected Councillor, 94

Pettitt, Richard, elected Mayor, 21; sworn, 22; made a Justice of the Peace, 35; death and burial of, 69

Philosophy Act in the Schools, 44

Piercey, Francis, elected Mayor, 121

Pillory, 10

Pindar, Mr, Pembroke College, preaches sermon before the Mayor, &c., at St Edward's Church, 23

Plague of London, 14, 15

Poll for Esquire Bedell, 81

Poor Man's Box, 7

Portreeves of the City of London, 119, 120

Potter, Samuel, elected Councillor, 93

Prychard, Humfry, Porter at Trinity College, 8

Pullen, Benjamin, junior Bursar at Trinity College, 54

140 INDEX.

Puller, Mr, Jesus College, preaches Alderman Ewin's funeral Sermon, 26
Pyke, Amy, death of, 82
Pyke, Alderman Henry, nominated Ensign of the Militia, 104; dies in prison, 110
Pyke, John, Town Clerk, death and burial of, 118
Pyke, Joseph, quarrels with Alderman Thomas Fox, *jun.*, and is stabbed by him, 117, 118; elected Alderman, 121; Mayor, 122; has a cancer in his mouth, 123
Pyke, Richard, 22
Pyke, Richard, death of, 61
Pyke, Thomas, death and burial of, 105.

Quarter Sessions, 25, 32, 40, 49, 60

Ramsey, James, death of, 94
Randall, Mr, elected Alderman, 128
Ranewes, Alderman, Obit sermon, 40
Ray, Richard, Butler of Trinity College, death of, 85
Reach Fair, 46
Read, Mr, marries Susanna Harrison, 111
Remery, Richard, Bailiff of the City of London, 120
Reynolds, Philip, Butler of St John's College, death and burial of, 121
Rhodes, Barbara, death of, 27
Rhodes, John, Prebendary of Norwich, death of, 22
Richardson, Purbeck, Esquire Bedell, commits suicide, 84
Richardson, Samuel, Bailiff, 2, 13, 22
Richardson, Samuel, lease of Harper's Booths in Sturbridge Fair granted to, 39

Ridgewell, Robert, 4
Rippington, Thomas, of Wentworth makes his will, 25
Rix, Samuel, death of, 52
Robbery by two scholars, one of Sidney and the other of Emmanuel, 53
Robson, James, elected Chief Constable, 32; death of, 75
Roderick, Dr Charles, elected Provost of King's, 102; admitted Provost, 104; Vice Chancellor, 121; death and burial of, 124
Rose, Christopher, elected Alderman, 3
Rule, Ralph, Bailiff, 2
Rumbold, William, elected Alderman, 117; Mayor, 119

St John's College, Lease of ground granted to, 38
Samburne, Mr, Master of the Ceremonies at the visit of the Prince of Orange, 59
Sancroft, Abp., resigns the Chancellorship of the University, 101
Sanders, ( ), Lease granted to, 51
Sanders, James, Freeman, 45
Sanderson, elected Treasurer, 26
Sanderson, N., elected Professor of Mathematics, 123
Sawyer, Nathaniel, Carrier, brings the news of the acquittal of the Bishops to Cambridge, 95
Sawyer, Sir Robert, chosen representative at the Westminster Convention, 98
Schools, Philosophy Act in the, 44; Bp Wren's body taken to the, 18
Sclater, Sir Thomas, Freeman, 57
Scott, Ann, death of, 82
Scott, Mr, elected a Senior Fellow of Trinity College, 72

Scott, Mr, Sidney College, preaches Sarah Simpson's funeral sermon, 83
Scott, Nicholas, death of, 76
Scott, Robert, Senior Fellow of Trinity College, death of, 108
Scrimshaw, Jane, aged 127 years, 123
Sergeant, Mr, King's College, preaches Richard Chevin's Obit sermon, 41
Sergeson, Mr, preaches sermon before the Mayor, &c., at St Edward's Church, 22
Settle, Peter, elected Councillor, 93
Shaw, Mr, St John's College, a Candidate for the Representation of the University, 122
Shepherd, Samuel, elected M.P. for Cambridge, 122; enlarges the Town Mace, 123
Sheriffs of London, 120
Sheward, Catherine, death of, 70
Sickness, 13, 15, 16
Simpson, Robert, Fellow of Caius College, elected Esquire Bedell, 128
Simpson, Rowland, sends present to the Mayor, 8; Auditor, 11; elected Alderman, 13; death and burial of, 24
Simpson, Sarah, death and burial of, 83
Skeiring, Mr, elected Alderman, 93
Sky, Fiery appearance of the, 16
Smith, Dr, Rector of Cottenham, death and burial of, 127
Smith, John, of Bene't parish, Councillor, death of, 56
Smithson, Mr, Fellow of Christ's College, his reported appointment to the Mastership, 95
Somerset, Charles, Duke of, elected Chancellor of the University, 101

Southwark, fire at, 21
Spalding, Mrs, Relict of Alderman Spalding, death of, 57
Spalding, Alderman Samuel, death of, 55
Sparkes, Edward, appointed Master of the Perse School, 90
Sparkes, Elizabeth, death of, 89
Sparkes, John, joins the Fleet at Harwich, 12
Sparkes, John, death of, 86
Spence, Benjamin, Freeman, 35
Spencer, Dr John, Master of Bene't College, death and burial of, 107
Spencer, Mrs, wife of Dr Spencer, Master of Bene't College, dies from Small Pox, and is buried the same night, 72
Stagg, John, Manciple, 55
Stamford, Mr, of Christ's, appointed Minister for Sturbridge Fair, 49
Stedman, Mr, elected a Senior Fellow of Trinity, 70
Sterne, Edward, executed for robbery, 10
Stevens, Dr, death of, 75
Stillingfleet, Dr, *sen.*, preaches at Gt St Mary's Church, 27; takes his D.D. Degree, 27
Stillingfleet, Dr, *jun.*, preaches at Gt St Mary's Church, 27; takes his D.D. Degree, 27
Storm, 16, 114
Story, Edward, Justice of the Peace, 75, 93; receives the Sacrament as Justice of the Peace, 76
Story, Captain Edward, death of, 107
Story, Elizabeth, death of, 89
Stoyt, Dr Edward, death and burial of, 114
Stubbe, Dr Wolfran, elected Regius Professor of Hebrew, 95
Sturbridge Fair, 2; not held on ac-

count of the Plague of London, 15; proclaimed, 31, 51; Regulators appointed, 50; Lease of Harper's Booths in, granted to Sam. Richardson, 39

Sturgeon, 78

Syke, Dr H., Professor of Hebrew, commits suicide, 124

Symonds, ( ), elected Councillor, 94

Symons, William, 95

Tabor, Mrs, wife of Nicholas Tabor, death of, 21

Taylor, ( ), elected Councillor, 94

Tempest, 16

Terry, Thomas, convicted of forgery, 17

Thamar, Mr, Organ builder, 81

Thames frozen over, 87

Thanksgiving, Public, 98

Thompson, James, a free Burgess, 115

Thompson, Roger, marries Mrs Anne Margery, 26

Thompson, Roger, Baptism of, 41

Thompson, Thomas, elected Councillor, 94

Thunder in February, 71

Thurloe, ( ), Wife of Peter Thurloe, dies from the Sickness, 16

Tillett, Titus, 36

Tindale, Dr William, Trinity Hall, death and burial of, 124

Tower of London, The King's Crown, Sceptre, &c., stolen from, 60

Townsend, Bailiff, 13

Townsend, Mr, Treasurer, 11

Townsend, Mr, elected Councillor, 28

Townsend, Mr, Lease of the Mills granted to, 39

Townsend, John, elected Bailiff, 22

Townsend, John, elected Alderman, 93

Trinity College, deaths arising from falling down stairs in, 8, 16, 72

—— ——, yearly allowance to the Auditor, 54

Tudway, Mr, removed from his Post of Organist at Pembroke College, but is restored again, 117

Turner, Judge, holds the Assizes at Cambridge, 62

Turner, Mr, Freeman, 59

Tuscany, Prince of, arrives at Cambridge, 43; his reception, 43, 44

Urlin, Mr, preaches sermon before the Mayor, &c., 63

Valentine, James, Trinity College, dies from the effects of a fall down stairs, 16

Vere, Albericus de, Portreeve of the City of London, 120

Vintner, William, Freeman, 27

Waits, The, 7, 50, 57, 62, 101

Wales, Prince of, Son of James II., birth of, 95

Walker, William, Apothecary, created Doctor in Physic by the King's mandate, 92

Walles, Gilman, enters Pembroke College, 119

Walls Lane, 50, 52

Washington, Mr, Minister of Little St Mary's, preaches funeral sermon of James Fletcher, the Mayor, 115

Watlington, Isaac, Mayor, 91; marries Mrs Dorothy Dillingham (his fourth wife), 105; death of, 111

Watlington, Mr, elected Alderman, 96

Watson, Thomas, of Ely, marries Margaret Cole, 57

Webb, Francis, elected Town Clerk, 93
Welbore, John and Philip, 59
Welbore, Philip, death of, 74
Welbore, Susanna, death of, 57
Wells, Dr, Master of Queens' College, death and burial of, 74
Wells, Susannah, wife of Alderman Wells, death, burial, and funeral sermon of, 8
Wells, Alderman William, marries Jane Allen, 16; death of, 21
Wendy, James, elected Councillor, 93
Wendy, Thomas, elected Councillor, 93
West, Nicholas, elected Treasurer, 12
Westminster Convention, 97, 98
Wheeler, Sir Charles, elected M.P. for the University, 17
Whiskin, Mr, elected Alderman, 128
Whiston, W., Professor of Mathematics, expelled from the University, 123, 124
Whitlock, Mrs. Mary, death and burial of, 127
Whitchcott, Dr Benjamin, death of, 85
Whybrow, Thomas, Vicar of Impington, death and burial of, 52
Whyn, Mr, University Registrar, 36
Wickham, Mr, preaches Alderman Pedder's funeral sermon, 25
Widdington, Dr, Fellow of Christ's College, elected Lady Margaret Professor of Divinity, 70; death of, 94
Wigmore, Dr Gilbert, death and burial of, 83
Wilford, Francis, Master of Bene't College, Vice-Chancellor, death of, 21

Wilford, Mrs, widow of the late Vice-Chancellor, death of, 24
William and Mary, Proclamation of, 98—101
William III. visits Cambridge; his reception there, 103, 104; death of, 112
Williams, Philip, Auditor, 11; elected Alderman, 26; Lease of the Mills granted to, 39; elected Mayor, 50, 52; death of, 74
Williams, (   ), Freeman, 73
Wilson, Edward, elected Alderman, 24; resignation of, 62; death of, 91
Wilson, John, elected Alderman and Mayor, 128
Winchester, Roger, Bailiff of the City of London, 120
Wind, Storm of, 114, 125
Windham, Judge, holds the Assizes at Cambridge, 42
Windsor, Hon. Mr, elected M.P. for the University, 122
Witham, John, elected Treasurer, 26
Wolgarius, Portreeve of the City of London, 119
Womack, Dr, Sub-Dean of Ely, 76
Worts, Mary, wife of William Worts, death and burial of, 114
Worts, William, Caius College, elected Esquire Bedell, 56; death and burial of, 114
Worts, William, son of William Worts, Esquire Bedell, death and burial of, 114, 181
Wren, Matthew, Bp of Ely, dies at Ely House, in London, 17; his body brought to Cambridge and placed in the Schools, 18; order of the Procession at the funeral in Pembroke College Chapel, 19, 20
Wrangle, Edward, 119

Wright, Dr. C., Professor of Arabic, death and burial of, 123

Wright, Sir Robert, Lord Chief Justice, death of, 101

Wyndham, Judge, holds the Assizes at Cambridge, 17

Wybrow, John, marries Margaret Calfe, 108

Young, Benjamin, marries Elizabeth Watlington, 109; Justice of the Peace, 113

York, Duke and Duchess of, visit Cambridge, 57

York, Duchess of, visits Cambridge, 79, 80

Printed in Dunstable, United Kingdom